PRAISE BE

E.H.

Copyright © 2020 Peanut Prints
All rights reserved.
ISBN: 978-0-6485460-2-3

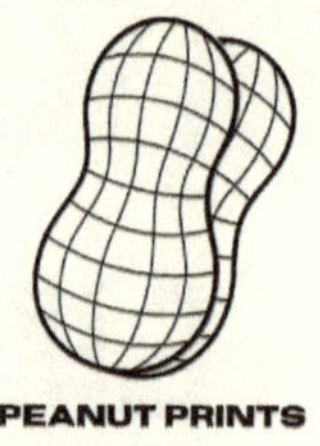

1

An afternoon passed; heavy grey clouds hung suspended in the breathless sky. Everything was quiet and still, and as Ricky slumped himself on his couch after work he cracked open a tinnie and sighed.

After years of living alone he'd grown some bad habits: the sink was always filled with dishes, and the sides and cracks around the tiles and sink In his bathroom were caked with grime. He always told himself he'd get around to cleaning it when he got the chance, but he rarely did. When he did clean something, he wouldn't maintain it, and after a few days his place would look exactly the same as it had before he tidied up.

He'd been married once, but it only lasted a couple of years. His missus left him because she said he lacked drive in anything. It took him a long time to get over that. Memories from their divorce would flash past him at least once a day still, but by now he'd learned how to control the feelings that he felt inside when he remembered.

He took a sip of beer as he sat quietly, listening to his kitchen clock tick. It was sunset, but he couldn't hear any birds out. The trees were dead still, and all that could be heard was the distant barking of dogs, or a loud motorbike echoing through the quiet suburban roads.

But suddenly the tranquility was shattered by the first breath of an oncoming storm, sweeping through the streets and rattling his windows violently.

"Fuck me dead!" he said to himself, looking out towards the approaching storm. He could see the ocean from his living room window, now looking like an expanse of grey mountain ranges, crashing and reforming in the distance, and as the rain began to bucket down he closed the rest of the windows in his house and put an old jumper on.

The storm was directly above him now, and as the lightning cracked over his house its blue light flashed in his peripheral vision and made him feel happy to be inside. He sat by the window and watched the rain spray against it in the wind, and mused how just a thin pane of glass could separate him from such a powerful storm. All of nature's might blocked by a sliver of glass. He didn't believe that nature was weak, not at all. Before his knee surgery he had surfed every day. He'd been worked by waves so many times that he had a distinct respect for nature, but now in his older age he could feel himself getting weaker, and it comforted him to think that something as fragile as a window could hold a powerful storm at bay.

He woke early for work the next morning and raced out in the rain to his van. At the entrance of the factory he was met by Phillip, the biggest cuck he'd ever met. Phillip was one of those guys that was way too happy to be at work; it made Ricky suspicious. Phillip would always laugh too loud at jokes, or his eye contact would linger so long that it would make Ricky feel uncomfortable. He always wondered if maybe Phillip had a double life of debauchery and filth — he was too good of a person to not have something fucked up about him. He found it hard to place what exactly made him feel that way, but nevertheless, he couldn't stand Phillip.

"Here he is!" said Phillip when he spotted Ricky running through the rain.

"Fuck off, Phillip…" Ricky muttered.

Phillip laughed. He thought that he and Ricky had a long-running inside joke where Ricky would always tell him to get fucked; he never saw him do it to anyone else. In his head, he and

Ricky shared the closest form of workplace camaraderie there was: friendly insults.

"What's the bet that today I'm gonna stack faster than you again?" Phillip smirked as he followed Ricky to the locker room.

"I'll let ya know when I start caring..."
"Yeah, yeah! You don't care 'cus you keep losing!" Phillip laughed.

They got changed into their work clothes and headed into the factory.

"How about that storm last night, huh? Was really something..." said Phillip as they walked.

"Yeah... Nearly blew my bloody windows off."

"They're pretty amazing when you think about it, storms, that is. Just another way that God shows us he's still there."

"Fuck me... just when I thought you couldn't get any more irritating."

Phillip stopped, and for the first time ever Ricky saw anger on his face. "Why? Because I believe in God? What do you believe in, Ricky? Aye? A six-pack and a two-hundred-dollar prostitute?"

"Fuck me dead, calm down, you're gonna give yourself a headache. And how do you know how much a prostitute costs?"

"I don't, it was a guess. But I'm sick and tired of the way you treat me, all I ever do is show you respect."

Ricky considered for a moment. "Yeah, nah, you're right, Phil, you're not that much of a dickhead."

Before Phillip had a chance to reply, Turbo, the packing captain, spotted them and called the pair over to the group meeting.

Turbo was a strange character. His real name was James, but he hated being called by it. James was his father's name, an upright, stiff-backed barrister who Turbo had always despised for his audacity in naming his son after himself. His whole life Turbo had been forced to study, play music and dance. He was forced to achieve, and the day he turned eighteen he vowed to himself that he'd never achieve anything in his father's eyes again. He earned the name Turbo from his schoolmates after he drank a whole case of lager and spewed up all over a girl he was kissing. He loved the name, it reminded him of everything his father wasn't. But somehow, after all his purposeful underachieving, he had still been made team packing captain.

"Just a few announcements this morning and then I'll let yas get back to work," he began.

"Firstly, everyone say happy birthday to Steven, it's his forty-fourth birthday today."

The team gave a half-hearted hurray, before Andy the forklift driver remarked, "Looks like he didn't get any more hair for his birthday again this year!" and everyone in the circle laughed.

A moment later Turbo continued. "Secondly, the people in the office are starting to complain. As you might know, the company is startin' to go into liquidation, so they're gettin' tighter and tighter with their money, and they reckon they've caught one of you on camera sneaking a few biscuit packets out of the damaged boxes and they want me to fire the culprit."

The circle grew tense. *Everyone* had been stealing biscuit packets.

But Turbo didn't notice the change in mood, and moved on uncaringly. "Lastly, whoever's not cleaning the fuckin' toilet bowl in the men's bathrooms is a grub. No one wants to look at your skid marks, so clean it up!"

This lightened the mood, and as Turbo finished, Andy the forklift driver was wearing a wry smile on his face that as good as told everyone that he was the culprit.

Turbo turned and shuffled back into his bare brick office in the corner of the factory. He had a massive hangover and needed to recover from it in silence.

The rest of the team got to work.

The factory was split up into three different sections. There was the labelling row, the stacking row and the collection row. Ricky and Phillip were both on the stacking row, stacking one box on to another until they were ready to be collected by cross-country trucks that drove the biscuits to supermarkets all across the nation.

Ricky hated the job. After he'd finished school his only plan was to surf and party. A few years later he ran out of money, and no girls wanted to sleep with him because he was out of shape and rough looking from the years of excessive drinking, drugs and lack of sleep. He'd been at the factory for almost fifteen years. Some would see it as an accomplishment, sticking at a job for that long, but the thought scared him every day. He'd always watch the older guys that had been working at the factory for decades. The long years of arduous stacking in silence had made them loopy, and often he'd walk past them and hear them muttering to themselves. He always wondered what they were muttering about, until he realised that while he was thinking about it he was muttering too. He felt like the biscuit factory was gripping him tighter every day, but he just lacked the drive to look for different work. He always felt like his freedom was just around the corner, but he guessed that's how you made any man willingly spend his life doing something he disliked.

By the end of the day the rain had finally started to clear, and as the sunlight broke through the clouds Ricky could smell the evaporating moisture in the air. It was a sweet smell that always reminded him of his spring holidays from school as a kid. When the smell of blooming flowers was strong in the air and the harsh Australian sun began to sting instead of warm.

He used to run down to the beach to surf every day on the turn of summer, and all he could hear were the sounds of crashing waves in the distance and the swarms of cicadas roaring under the belting heat.

He was shaken out of his daydream by the roar of a truck, and the ceaseless groaning of the conveyor belts that carried an endless stream of biscuit packets.

The clock struck three-thirty, which was the end of his shift. Turbo appeared from out of his office to see everyone off, and somehow, he looked even rougher than he had earlier in the morning.

"Great work everyone, you're all smashing it," he said unenthusiastically as the team filed one by one into the changing rooms, but before Ricky got the chance to slip through, Turbo stopped him.

"Hey, Ricky, I need to talk to you for a minute if that's alright?"

"Yeah, Turbo, no worries," said Ricky, more politely than usual.

He wasn't scared of Turbo, and he wasn't a suck-up either, but there was something in Turbo's tone that made him worried.

They walked into Turbo's office and he closed the door behind him.

"How you been, mate?" Turbo asked Ricky as he sat down.

"Yeah, been alright, not much to tell really, you?"

"Been good, man, but let's get to why I asked you to come in here," Turbo replied as he took a seat.

Turbo leaned in on his chair and took a deep breath. "You're the one they caught on camera stealing those biscuit packets." Ricky went to defend himself but Turbo raised his hand. "Look, man, I'm not blaming you. I know everyone steals the biscuits – shit, even I steal the biscuits – but if they catch you again I'm gonna have to let you go."

It pained Turbo to talk to someone like that; it reminded him of his unwanted authority, and if he hadn't been in need of a stable income he would have left the biscuit factory the moment they promoted him.

Ricky nodded his head. "Won't happen again, Turbo, promise."

Turbo raised his hands. "Aye, all I said was don't get caught…"

With nothing more to discuss, Ricky stood up and left the office, and as he closed his door behind him Turbo sighed in relief.

Sometimes we leave places with no intent of ever returning. Every day that thought crossed Ricky's mind when he started his car and drove away from the factory, but he knew he would come back. There was nowhere else for him to go. He felt like a moth drawn to an electric zapper, and every time he went near he was zapped just a little bit more into submission.

He drove straight to the beach that afternoon. It was early autumn, and the ocean was still warm enough to swim in comfortably. He wasted no time in getting into his swimmers before hobbling over the sand and diving straight into the water without feeling the temperature first. The touch of the ocean on his skin cleaned more than just the sweat and grime that he'd collected throughout his day of work, and as he resurfaced he cupped his hands against his face and wiped the water away from his eyes and nose.

He smiled to himself at the simple beauty of it all. The waves were gentle, even though the night before he had seen the grey mountains crashing and churning at the very spot he was now swimming, and so he lay on his back and floated for a while, watching the clouds pass in the sky above.

He never felt alone in the ocean. It was one place where all the elements balanced themselves into perfect company, and when he looked out at the soft horizon that blended into the sea in the distance he felt as if he was gazing at an old friend.

He'd been in the ocean almost every day for his entire life. Every day after school he had raced to the beach, even during school he surfed, slipping out at lunchtimes and not coming back for the rest of the day. Those were treasured memories.

The rush of seeing a mountainous wave forming in the distance and turning your board around to paddle for it. The wind rushing past your ears as you flew down the face of the wave, racing to dodge the whitewash that crashed behind you just to pull up and turn back again. It was one great balancing act, and one that was dependent on the timing and grace that was learned from flowing with the wave. If you try too hard you were guaranteed to fall, but not trying at all was where the danger lay.

He dove under the water and held his breath for a while, listening to the salt and sand crackling in his ears as he glided just above the bottom. He opened his eyes and imagined himself floating over a vast desert, but after too short a time he lost his breath and was forced to return to the surface. There was something about being underwater that he couldn't put his finger on, some deep, soothing calmness that the ocean possessed. It reminded him of his mother. He remembered her always as wearing flowing dresses adorned with flowers. She was the most beautiful woman he'd ever known, and the most caring and kind. But she was fierce. He remembered the way her graceful features could turn as hard as stone within an instant, and back to graceful the next. She was unpredictable and strong, just like the ocean.

He hadn't known his father well; he ran away with another woman when Ricky was just a boy. He guessed that's why his mother was so protective, but as he grew older she saw his father in him more and more. The only memory he had of his father was that every Sunday morning he would sit with Ricky on his lap and read the newspaper. Ricky would pretend to read it with him, but all he'd do was look at the pictures, or lose himself in daydreams.

Those were just distant memories now, but he held them close to his heart.

The world was changing quickly, and Ricky felt like he was falling behind more and more. Gone were the days where all the boys would have piss-ups on the job. Gone were the days where you could have a good old-fashioned blue at the local pub and have no consequences with the law, and more often than not you'd end up having a beer with the same bloke you punched on with. The days when the pub had its own law, based on honour and what it meant to be a good bloke. Those were good days, sunny days, filled with camaraderie and brotherhood.

Now Ricky thought everyone was too focused on safety and productivity, to the point where he felt like he couldn't even take a shit at work without some stiff-backed manager with a clipboard timing him.

Ricky hated that those days were gone, and as the years passed and he was taken further and further away from those glory days he became bitter with everything and everyone. Nothing made sense to him anymore... shitty drivers, incompetent people and downright idiots, all of whom he felt like he had to dodge every day just to get a bottle of milk and some bread.

He was frustrated with the world, and he was frustrated with the direction it was heading.

But he knew there was nothing he could do to change its course, so he drank every night with his mates, and woke up each morning groaning with a hangover.

2

The next morning, he arrived at work to find a group of men and women wearing business clothes waiting with Turbo for everyone to arrive. They eyed him as he entered the factory, and they did their best to maintain their authoritative look, but Ricky could see the discomfort on their faces. They weren't accustomed to the ceaseless groaning of the conveyor belts, or the crunching and crashing of empty pallets under the weight of the mechanical crusher. He greeted them with a silent nod, and joined the group. Another ten minutes passed before Phillip and the rest of the team arrived and completed the circle.

Turbo stepped forward in his usual manner to address the team. "Morning, everyone. This morning's team meeting's gonna be a little different today. Behind me you've probably noticed Richard and his team from the head office with us today – they've come to say a few words."

Without further prompting, Richard stepped forward. He was a middle-aged man with slicked-back hair and pointy shoes, and as he began his speech Ricky could tell he'd said it a hundred times before.

"Thanks for that, James. Good morning, team. For those of you that don't know already, the company has fallen on hard times during the recent economic crash. We've tried our hardest to do right by our staff, and to do right by our investors. At the end of the day, we're a family business. We care so deeply about our staff, and they are engrained into our very culture. But, unfortunately, we've had to make the tough decision to close this factory down. There simply isn't enough revenue coming through that could justify us keeping this branch open. From all of us at Biscuit Co, we're terribly sorry, and we wish you all the best."

No one could find the words to respond. They were all so shocked by the abruptness of the whole thing.

The team stood in silent disbelief for a few moments more before Andy the forklift driver blurted out angrily, "Family business? What a fuckin' load of shit!"

Richard raised his hand. "I understand your feelings, but please don't swear at us."

Phillip was pale in the face, and as he spoke his voice almost quivered. "Please, I have a family to look after! Surely there is something you can do for all of us?"

Richard smiled in an attempt at empathy, but Ricky saw indifference in his eyes. "After a lot of meetings and discussions, we all agreed to pay out to all of you two weeks' worth of wages. That's all we can do."

Ricky couldn't believe it. Richard and his posse of office workers left the factory, leaving the team in silence.

In a way Turbo was happy; he'd always hated the job, but had been too lazy to look for another one. Now he'd have to. He felt bad for everyone else, though. He stepped forward again and addressed the team for the last time. "Well, I'm sorry, guys, there's not much I can say. It's been a pleasure workin' with you all."

"Argh piss off, you lazy fuck!" said Andy, before turning around and storming out of the factory.

The group dispersed, talking quietly amongst themselves, troubled by the road ahead.

At the entrance Phillip caught up to Ricky. "Fuck me! What are we all gonna do now?"

"I dunno, Phil. Can't you just pray for another job?" said Ricky. He wasn't in the mood to listen to Phillip whinge.

Phillip stopped. "You know what? Get fucked, Ricky. I've only ever shown you respect and all I've ever got in return is your bullshit. Have a nice life, asshole."

Ricky felt like he'd been backhanded. Being fired was one thing, but copping a spray from Phillip pushed him over the edge.

"Yeah, nah, whatever, mate," said Ricky, before giving Phillip the finger and getting into his car.

As he drove away, he looked back at the factory one last time through the rearview mirror and saw Phillip standing there watching him drive into the distance. As he drove he breathed in and out heavily, and his hands shook from adrenaline. On that day both his biggest hope and greatest fear had come true. He was free of the biscuit factory, and free of Phillip, but now he had no income and his bills would pile up.

He drove straight to the headland, recklessly turning corners and speeding down quiet side streets before he screeched to a stop at the headland.

He got out of the car and slammed the door, and without any regard for anyone else around he tore his way through the shrubbery on top of the headland until he reached the edge of the cliff where he roared at the top of his lungs, "FUUCK!"

His legs felt like lead. He slumped himself down against a rock and stared out silently over the horizon. Despite his mood, it was a beautiful day. Not a cloud was in the sky and the warm autumn sun shimmered over the ocean; he winced against its brightness as he peered out.

"Are you ok?" asked a soft voice behind Ricky.

"Fuck off," he replied.

He heard footsteps coming carefully towards him, and the next moment a young woman in her mid-twenties sat by his side.

She was beautiful. Her hair was golden brown, bleached from the sun and salt, and her skin was bronzed and shiny. Her eyes were a bluey-green colour, just like the ocean.

His heart was pounding, but it wasn't because of losing his job anymore.

"What's your name?" she asked, smiling.

"What's it to you?" he replied, remembering his temper.

"I heard you yelling, and thought I'd come and see if you were ok?"

"I'm not gonna jump, if that's what you were wondering."

She smiled, "I didn't think you would, but what are you doing yelling up here? You gave me a fright."

Ricky raised his head and looked at her, and all of a sudden he felt like a child having a tantrum. "Just got laid off from work. Figured I needed to let off some steam..."

"I'm sorry to hear that," she replied.

"Nah, you're alright, I'm sorry for telling you to fuck off, been a bad day."

"I understand, it sucks when life throws those things at you. Sometimes all we need is a little faith to get us through the day," she replied.

"Yeah, but I don't have faith in anything, not even myself," said Ricky, feeling sorry for himself.

He felt her hand touch his shoulder, as light and gentle as a feather. "You have a lot to be faithful in. Do you live locally?" she asked.

"Yeah, yeah, just live round the corner from here actually," he said, turning around as if to point his house out.

"That's great, I live around here too. I know this sounds a little weird, we've only just met, but you should come over for dinner one night this week. We can talk some more then if you'd like. I've got to get going, is all," she said, looking at her phone.

Ricky didn't know what to say, so taken aback was he by the whole situation and by her beauty, but after a few awkward moments he managed to blurt out, "Yeah, sure."

"Great. Does tomorrow night work for you?"

"Yeah, sounds good, not like I have a job to cancel my plans for anyways," he laughed.

She took out a piece of paper and a pen from her handbag and scribbled down her phone number before giving it to Ricky. "See you tomorrow," she said, and turned to leave.

Ricky looked down at the piece of paper. Her name was written on the top in graceful, educated handwriting: *Emma*.

He mouthed her name as he read. He'd never met a woman as beautiful as her, and not just in a physical sense. She radiated calmness and intelligence. Next to her he felt like a bull of a man, totally untrained in etiquette and in the tone that carried all of the white-collar conversations he'd ever overheard.

He sat upon the headland for a while longer and peered out into the horizon. The waves crashed against the rocks below, and above him the seabirds darted and dove through the air like acrobats on a trapeze.

Meeting Emma made him feel a little better, but he still burned with frustration, and it could only be stifled by going to the pub and drowning his troubles with a couple of schooners.

That evening Ricky rolled into his local pub, the Crystal Palace, and sat down at his usual spot with a group of the local patrons.

"Here he is! Heard ya got the sack, big dog," bellowed Alph, a red-faced, loudmouthed old boy that practically lived at the pub. He was one of those blokes that was constantly full of tall stories and outrageous lies. He lied with so much conviction that he almost believed them himself. He was in the pub every day without fail: in the afternoons he'd sit at the pokie machines and slap through fifty-dollar notes back to back until the rest of the boys showed up, and at night he'd drink. Ricky had watched him use the pokie machines for so many years, he always wondered if Alph was either filthy rich, or just terrible with money. He reckoned he was terrible with money, but he could never tell. Alph was always dipping off on small getaway trips to Indonesia so he'd have to have had some money. Back in the day, Alph used to be the law out in the water. He was renowned and feared for both his skill in surfing and his willingness to punch on with anyone who didn't look local. There was a rumour that one time a thirteen-year-old grom dropped in on Alph's wave, and afterwards Alph chased him down the beach and locked him in a dog cage before pissing on him. Regardless of how true the stories were, he wasn't someone you'd want to get in the way of.

The rest of the boys laughed and patted Ricky on the back as he sat down at the table.

"Bunch of fuckin' cunts they are," said Ricky, and with a single sip he downed half of his beer.

"Who's that?" asked Codge, another of the patrons, just as loud and drunk as Alph.

"The fuckin' cunts in the office. They come down into the factory all fuckin' stiff-backed, like they reckon they own the place and without hesitating they sack the whole fuckin' team."

"Bunch of dogs..." said Alph darkly, and the rest of the table grunted in agreement.

Around the table there was Ricky, Alph, Damo and Codge. The four of them had been drinking at the Crystal Palace almost every day for twenty years. They'd been going there for so long that often it felt as if the dingy carpet and the sticky table were as homely to them as their own living rooms.

Codge patted Ricky on the back, he could tell Ricky was devastated. "It's ok, Rick, you'll get another job. Fuck me, you hated that place anyway, could be the biggest blessing in the end."

Ricky took another gulp of beer and placed his empty glass back on the table. "Yeah, you're probably right. Just gets to me the way those office people were."

"Yeah, Codgey's right... fuck 'em Rick! You're better off without 'em!" said Alph.

Damo stood up. He was a quiet guy who always wore a pair of thick, dark, wraparound sunglasses, no matter where he was or what time of day it was.

"I'm gettin' a beer, what you want, Ricky? On me, big fella..."

Ricky smiled at him appreciatively. "Just grab us a schooner."

Damo nodded and shuffled off towards the bar. Ricky's friends would never offer him a shoulder to cry on, but they'd pick him up and tell him to stop being a sook, and he was thankful every day for it.

He remembered the day his missus left him. He rocked up to the Crystal Palace almost in tears and, after he had told the boys what happened, Alph put his hand on Ricky's shoulder and said, "Come on, mate, you're makin' the rest of us miserable too."

Ricky laughed, and all the boys patted him on the back. That was a night he'd never forget. He stayed up until three in the morning, drunk and yelling his sorrows at the moon out on the headland.

The pub was one of the few places besides the ocean where he felt comfortable. The constant clinging and chatter in the background made it easy to talk and feel as if he had privacy, and after a few drinks he loosened up and felt more open to the world.

There was one topic that the boys never failed to talk about when they met up, and that was sex. They loved sizing up every girl they saw at the pub. Alph would always nod his head and raise his eyebrows every time an attractive girl walked past their table, and like a group of owls, all of their heads would cock to the side and follow her as she walked by. Ricky couldn't count how many times he'd seen someone stop mid-sentence just to stare at a girl's ass. Ricky loved women too. But not the degrading way they did, it always made him feel a little uncomfortable when the boys did that. And even though he did it with them, it was only so they wouldn't ask questions. Alph and Damo loved prostitutes.

Their outlook on sex was purely money based. In their eyes paying a prostitute for sex was the same, if not cheaper, than taking a girl out on a few dates to get the same outcome. Ricky loved sex, but he loved it more because of its emotional sensations. Ricky had been with a lot of women, and he'd had a lot of different kinds of sex. He'd had sex with girls who were wild and free, shy girls, dominative girls, and submissive girls too. But to him, nothing beat the feeling of making love to someone that he cared about.

He remembered the first time he and his ex-wife slept with each other. They'd been in love with one another well before that evening. Ricky loved her from the moment he looked at her, and every time they found themselves near one another he could feel the gravitation between them. Asking her out on a date was a move so out of character that even he didn't know what he was doing. He just felt compelled to put it all on the line and ask her on a date. When she agreed he almost skipped home he was so happy.

Feeling like you know someone, and feeling completely comfortable with them before you finally sleep with one another is one of those few pure feelings you feel when you're an adult.

Lovey-dovey sex that's awkward and cute at the same time, because at that moment both of your wildest imaginations are coming true. You giggle as you pull each other's clothes off, and as you kiss, you smile and laugh, almost in disbelief that what's happening really is.

And afterwards, you hold each other close in silence, speaking without words and sounds, with little periods of eye contact, but mostly touch and feel. When you gently hold someone's arm in your hand, and you caress your thumb back and forth slowly against their skin.

Those moments were far more memorable to Ricky than the moments of wild, loveless sex. Loveless sex made him feel like an animal in the wild, reproducing out of primal necessity, making love made him feel human, and holding a woman gently against his body made him feel like a man.

Alph downed his beer and thumped it on the table triumphantly. "Fuck me, I'm keen for tomorrow."

"Yeah? What you got on?" asked Ricky, trying not to think of the biscuit factory.

"Goin' to Thailand, mate! Can't wait to get me leg over one of them young Thai birds."

"Bloody oath, the fuckin' rigs on 'em are phenomenal, I'm jealous, ya lucky bastard!" laughed Codge.

Ricky nodded his head in agreement. "Just don't come back with a wife, you grub."

"A wife? Fuck off, dog! I'll come back with two," laughed Alph.

"Gonna get my leg over something tomorrow too actually," said Ricky, remembering Emma.

"Fuck off you will, only thing you'd get a leg over is Madame Cecelia down at the doll house ya ugly cunt!" said Codge.

Ricky laughed and shook his head. "Met her this arvo, asked me to come round to hers tomorrow night. Gave me her number and all."

"Ah yeah? What's his name?" laughed Alph, and the two of them pretended to fight as they laughed.

But moments later a real fight ensued. Damo was walking back to the table holding the beers when a man bumped into him accidentally and spilt the drinks all over him. Damo looked at the man in disbelief and barked, "You better pay for those!"

The man wore a suit and had obviously just come home from working in the city. He looked at Damo in his wraparound sunglasses and sneered at him, "Fuck off, mate, should have looked where you were going."

The man's friends could sense the fight coming and they rose from their seats, but not before Damo leaned back as far as he could and king-hit the man in the jaw. The man collapsed instantly and his friends jumped on Damo like a pack of dogs, swinging madly in every direction. Not a moment after Ricky, Alph and Codge jumped in wielding chairs and glasses, and in an instant the Crystal Palace was host to an all-out pub brawl.

Ricky swung madly into the brawl, punching anyone he could see wearing a suit. He took some hits too – one of the younger men landed two solid shots to Ricky's right eye – but there was no way of getting him down. All of his frustration bubbled to the surface, turning him into a raging dog, foaming from the mouth and barking wildly. The fight spilled out into the street, and Ricky was punching up one of the suit wearers against a wall. It felt good to let his anger out. He felt his fist sink into the man's face over and over again until his knuckles were raw and bloody and then he suddenly stopped. The man he was holding was whimpering, blood gushing from his nose and lips. It was a pathetic sight. The man tried to run away but he was too disorientated and he stumbled over himself and landed flat on his face. Ricky watched on, and a feeling of disgust sank in his stomach. He felt ugly, and when he noticed his bloody knuckles he tried in vain to wash them off in the gutter.

He turned around and rushed home. He almost kicked his front door down, and he slammed it behind him on the way in. He was breathing heavily now, pacing up and down erratically until he walked into the bathroom and looked at himself in the mirror.

"Fuck you, cunt. FUCK YOU!" he yelled at himself. His right eye was bloodshot and watery from the punches.

He tore his way through his house, flipping over his dining-room table and punching holes in the paintings on the walls before stumbling to the kitchen and opening a bottle of rum. He collapsed onto the sofa and swigged out of the bottle as tears streamed down his face.

The moon was full that night, and its pale white light beamed through the living room window and onto Ricky as he lay there and drank.

Ten more minutes passed before he blacked out and dropped the bottle, but by then it was almost finished, and it rolled away.

3

The next day Ricky dragged himself to the beach. He lay on his back in the ocean, staring up at the sky in silence. He felt awful, physically and emotionally: the image of the man he beat senseless the night before kept flashing past him.

He closed his eyes and let himself drift above the surface, bobbing up and down gently with the ripples of swell that passed under him. As he floated he thought of his ex-wife, Eliza. He missed her a lot. In fact, not a day went past where she wasn't in the back of his mind. He'd tried everything to get over her, or at least to get through the pain of losing her, but nothing so far had helped him.

After his swim, he sat on the headland for a while and looked out at the clouds on the horizon. They were dark grey, and he could see the pillars of heavy rain falling from them in the distance. He took out his phone and dialed up Emma's number, holding his breath while the phone rang.

His heart stopped when she picked up. "Emma speaking."

He paused for a second, unsure of what to say, as if he'd never intended on calling her in the first place. After a few moments her voice came again in a puzzled "Hello?"

"Ah yeah, hi, Emma. It's Ricky, from the headland," he managed to blurt out.

"Ricky! A part of me thought you wouldn't call, but I'm happy you did. How are you?"

"Yeah, nah, I'm alright, just on the headland again, looking out at the big storm that's comin' in. I was just wonderin' if you were still keen on tonight?" he said, almost anxiously. He felt like a schoolboy asking his crush out to the movies.

"Of course!" she said. "Come round any time after six. I'll text my address."

He smiled in relief. "Sounds good, I'll see ya there," he finished and hung up. For the first time in a while he felt like a champion. His chest swelled with excitement and a moment later his phone pinged with a message from Emma containing her address and a smiley face.

She lived just around the corner from him. He looked at the time. It was four o'clock and he figured he'd better start getting ready. He walked home with a spring in his step, smiling as he looked up at the sun, which was quickly being overtaken by heavy clouds.

He got home and put on a playlist he found on his phone called 'Sex Music'. He hopped straight into the shower, where he washed his hair, shaved his stubble and trimmed his pubes while he hummed in tune with the music. He took out an old, grimy comb and gel and slicked his hair back. Afterwards he looked at the mirror and laughed at himself. Sometimes we do things so out of character that all we can do is laugh. He looked like the men he'd got in a fight with the night before, but he figured Emma would probably prefer them to what he was.

He ironed a white button-up shirt and dark denim pants and he slapped his neck with some old cologne his ex-wife had given to him as a Christmas present once. He told her it made him smell like a fuckwit, but now he felt like his life depended on the scent, and he was thankful for it.

He took the shirt off the iron and put it on, and the warmth of the freshly ironed cotton made him smile.

He turned the music up and pretended to dance a little as he paced through his house excitedly. He brushed his teeth and gargled mouthwash; he even flossed for the first time that he could remember in years. He felt smart, clean and sexy as he paced around the house, dusting off his old watch and a pair of sleek leather boots – another unused present from Eliza.

After almost an hour his transformation was complete, and when he stood in front of the mirror again he burst into hysterics. "Fuck me, you look a complete twat!" he laughed to himself. He just hoped that Emma wouldn't laugh. He tried to imagine a scenario where he'd knock on her door real smooth, and when she opened it the scent of his cologne would drift past her with the breeze and without a moment's hesitation he'd swoop her gracefully into his arms and they'd kiss deeply. That was the plan, anyway.

It was almost half past five when he began to feel the nerves kick in. They didn't creep up gradually, but hit all of a sudden, the feeling of impending doom sinking heavily in his stomach. His palms started sweating and it dawned on him that he was really going through with it. He hadn't been with another woman in years. After his divorce, he had wanted to stay as far away from them as possible, but there was something about Emma that made him feel compelled to see her.

He went back to the mirror again and looked at himself one last time. "Fuck me… you look a complete twat…" he repeated. This time there was panic in his voice, but it was too late to change, he already reeked of cologne and when he looked closer at the buttoned shirt it looked about ready to burst from the beer gut that pushed against it. He looked like a fat schoolboy on his first day of school. He used to bully kids that looked like him.

It was quarter to six now, and he knew he had to get going.

He picked up a bottle of wine from the kitchen and walked out hurriedly.

It was a five-minute walk to her house, but a part of him wished it were longer. It was ten to six by the time he arrived, but he wasn't sure if he was too early. He didn't want to come off as too eager, but he was already too close to turn back, and too early to knock on the door, so he waited just out of sight of her front window behind the next-door neighbour's front hedge.

He felt as if he was on some big prank show, and the whole world was watching him stumble around awkwardly.

"Ricky?" He heard a woman's voice behind him and his stomach sank. He whirled around and saw Emma walking towards him, holding a linen bag filled with groceries. He expected her to call him a creep or something for hiding behind the hedges but instead she walked up to him and smiled, "I'm so sorry! I thought I'd have enough time to duck to the shops quickly before you came."

Ricky smiled back. "Nah, you're alright, I only just got here myself." He could feel his heart thumping in his chest. She looked more beautiful than he remembered. Her hair was flowing, and she wore a loose floral dress that swayed gracefully in the breeze as she walked over to him. She gave him a friendly hug and a kiss on the cheek and he could smell her shampoo.

She led him to the front door before fumbling the key out of her handbag and unlocking it. Her house was simple by design. The walls were white and the wooden floorboards were a sandy brown colour that made him feel at home. It smelt of a department-store candle. There were a few simple black-and-white photos of trees on the walls, and a picture of an old broken-down beach van, but other than that the house was minimalistic.

Ricky stood in her living room awkwardly, not sure whether to strike conversation or to wait in silence as she ran around the house dropping her things off and putting her groceries in the fridge. She noticed him standing there and smiled warmly. "Take a seat, I'll be with you in a sec!"

He cleared the lump out of his throat and raised the bottle of wine he had brought to show Emma. "I brought this along, wasn't sure if you'd like it or not but figured it'd probably be polite."

"Thank you! You didn't need to bring this, but I'm glad you did," she said, and she took the bottle from him and grabbed two glasses from the cupboard.

Ricky was in deep thought. It had been so long since he'd been with a girl and he was trying to figure out how to make a move. The possibility of them having sex felt so far away to him now. In every romantic movie he'd seen he'd watched the man grab the girl from behind spontaneously, and all of a sudden they'd kiss passionately and things would go from there. But something in his stomach told him that was the wrong thing to do. In fact, the whole situation felt wrong to him somehow, but he couldn't place his finger on it.

Emma brought the glasses of wine to the table and sat down opposite Ricky.

They clinked their glasses and sipped, before Emma explained herself.

"I'm glad you came. You're probably super confused about why I asked you to come without knowing each other at all."

"Just figured it was on account of my good looks," joked Ricky, and Emma laughed.

"Of course, that too," she giggled, "but when I saw you on the headland yelling I couldn't help but approach you. I could feel the pain in your voice, and I knew that I was meant to talk to you."

"You could call it that I guess..." said Ricky, a little confused.

"Do you believe in God, Ricky?" she asked him, rather abruptly.

"You're fuckin' jokin'..." he thought to himself, but knowing better than to say that he shook his head instead. He knew this was too good to be true. Here he was thinking that he was finally going to have sex with someone, and the next thing he knows he's being asked if he believed in God. He wondered if maybe this was the worst foreplay ever, or more likely that there was no chance that Emma had asked him over to sleep with him.

"You don't need to believe in God to feel His presence," she said. "Why did you choose to go to the headland to yell?"

Ricky shrugged. "Dunno, just seemed like it'd be the right place."

Emma looked at him excitedly. "Don't you see? I know you can feel it. We belong with nature, that great balance, and you don't need to believe in God to know that."

"Yeah, nah, I suppose you're right," said Ricky, thinking of the ocean and how it made him feel closer to his mum. He'd never imagined it to be a sign of God. "Still doesn't make me believe in God but…" he said.

Emma smiled warmly. "Like I said before, you don't need to believe in God. When I saw you on the headland I knew that you needed saving. You were right on the edge of a cliff, and all you needed was someone to show you the way to the light. I don't believe in God in a religious sense. I believe in the oneness of everything. The waves crash and the wind blows, and all throughout there are fish that use the currents and birds that fly with the wind. That harmony, that oneness, to me is God."

"Yeah, but I eat those fish…" said Ricky.

"Exactly," said Emma, "and in time we die too, and by the same power you use to eat the fish, you too will be consumed. We use the universe's energy, and then we give it back."

"Fuck that, I'm not gettin' consumed," said Ricky, cheekily.

"It's just a part of life..." Emma replied.

Ricky paused for a moment and considered before he spoke again. "It sounds nice and all, the oneness of everything and the birds and the fish and that, but what's it got to do with me?"

Emma leant over the table and took his hand into hers; it was gentle and warm and her touch gave Ricky butterflies.

"Let me show you. I know you can feel the energy around you, I just think you need to feel it in yourself too," said Emma. "You don't have to do anything but listen to nature, be aware of it, open up to it and let it warm your heart. What is all around you is within, it's all a reflection of how you feel inside. Do you know what I mean?"

Ricky felt embarrassed, as if his mother or teacher were talking to him, and he wished that he had never come to Emma's house. But, deep down, he knew she was right.

Throughout all of his life's problems, he had always used the ocean to heal himself. He could feel the water wash away his grief, and the sun and salt vanquish his heartaches, but he never considered them to be as much a part of him as he was.

But, he wasn't ready yet, and although Emma's words were smooth and beautiful he resisted them because they were new and they required him to change his ways, and that scared him.

Suddenly he felt uncomfortable, and his hand recoiled from Emma's gentle touch. He stood. "I'm sorry... I gotta get going."

Emma smiled understandingly, and didn't push the subject any further. She walked him to the door and before he left she hugged him. "I want to see you again sometime. Is it ok if I message you again this week? We don't have to talk about God, we can just talk."

Ricky nodded, not having the strength to say no, and then he turned and left.

4

"So, you got all dressed up, made yourself smell like a poofter, just to talk about God!" Codge laughed at the Crystal Palace later on that night.

Ricky had gone straight to the pub from Emma's. He'd almost forgotten how he looked before Codge and the rest of the boys saw him. They were pissing themselves, so much so that old Codge was wiping tears away from his red face as he laughed.

"Yeah, yeah, go and get fucked, the lot of yas," laughed Ricky, waving them away with a flick of his hand.

"Where'd you get off to last night, anyways?" began Damo. "I was lookin' for you after the fight. Fuck me, it felt good to bash those dogs."

"Thought I saw a copper and ran for it," said Ricky, although he was lying. He didn't know why he felt like he had to lie, but the memory of him cursing at himself in the mirror flashed past him and he thought it was better not to share it.

"Nah, all good, we had to clear off as well anyways. Was just worried you'd got dragged off or somethin'," said Damo, before taking a sip from his schooner.

The boys sat around the table and drank as usual, talking about old school memories and old surf stories. Ricky remembered when he was eighteen and first started going to the pub with his mates. Back then he swore he'd never become an old patron. He would see them at every pub he went to. Old and worn out, drinking at the same table with the same friends, talking about the same things every night. But, the next thing he knew he was doing just that. He loved the pub, and he loved his friends, even if he would never tell them that out loud. The flashing lights from the pokie machines and the constant noisy chatter all around made him feel at home. His actual home was dark and empty, filled only with the sounds of his footsteps, or distant noises from the world outside.

There are very few kinds of people, and somehow, we all become one of them. Ricky knew which one of them he was, at least he could say that much.

He didn't stay long at the pub that night. The day he'd had had left a funny feeling in his stomach that he knew could only be fixed with a long walk.

Feeling a little tipsy, he stood up and said goodbye to the boys before leaving the bar.

On his walk home, he thought about what Emma had said about God and the oneness in everything.

The wind was cold and strong that night, but luckily it wasn't raining. As Ricky walked he stuffed his hands into his pockets and shivered.

He could hear the waves crashing far off in the distance; the sound travelled so much more easily at night. Nighttime was when the world listened. The animals of the night are blind. They listen, they smell and they feel, but they don't see. Just as the animals of the day are deaf. They see but they don't listen. Ricky never listened to anything in his life besides the groaning of the conveyor belts at the factory, but for some reason he had listened to Emma. There was something about her. He could have been in love, but it was a love he'd never experienced before. She was too pure for him to love. She reminded him of how he had been before. Before he became a man, before his heart was broken and he became numb to the world of women. He was always a goofy kid. He'd make everyone laugh with the faces he'd pull, and he would have never dreamed that one day he would be like this, and every day that passed he moved further away from that goofy kid, towards the archetype of the old boy at the pub, sinking beers and slapping his pay cheque into the pokie machines.

Two days passed before Ricky decided it was time to get out and look for another job. He had a week and a half's payout to go, and a tiny bit of money in savings after that, but he knew how quickly money went and he had begun to get worried.

He didn't know where to start. He'd worked at the biscuit factory so long that he'd forgotten the whole process of getting a job. He reckoned it wouldn't be that hard. Just a matter of walking into a place and asking to talk to the manager, and then he'd be in the money. He took out a nice button-up shirt and ironed it out, and around lunchtime he hopped into his van and drove into the city. He didn't have anywhere in mind, just the first place he saw with a 'We're Hiring' sign, or something like that. He was driving around the city centre for twenty minutes before he saw a sign out front of a café. He'd never worked hospitality before, but he figured that compared to the biscuit factory anything would be piss easy. He parked up and walked towards the entrance, and the closer he got the more nervous he got. He hated that he was in this position. He hated having to put himself out there and give a show, but he knew it was the only way he'd get a job fast.

The café was heaving, and as he stepped through the front door he immediately joined a seven-person queue.

"Fuck's sake," he muttered to himself. If there was one thing he hated more than anything it was waiting. To him, that was the biggest torture of all.

While he was in line he watched the waiters and waitresses rushing around the café manically, taking orders, bringing food and coffees, clearing plates and cleaning tables. They looked miserable. Their cheeks were red and occasionally he saw them stop to take a breather as if they'd just run a half-marathon. It looked more like a boot camp then a café. The hordes of hungry people kept waving their hands at the waiters and waitresses, or they'd whistle and call, and moments later a worn-out worker would be at their table with a pen and pad in hand. He was second in the queue when he overheard the woman in front of him complaining about her meal.

"I asked for gluten-free bread and you served me Turkish..." she began.

The poor woman at the counter looked so exhausted that she could hardly feign interest. "Oh my god, I'm so sorry about that!" she replied tonelessly.

The woman in the queue shook her head angrily. "That's not good enough. I want a full refund for my meal, otherwise I'll never come back here again, and I'll make sure none of my friends do, either."

"No worries, that's absolutely fine," began the woman behind the counter. "Please, help yourself to something from the display cabinet too while I sort out your refund."

The woman standing in the queue perked up at this and bent over the glass food cabinet eagerly. A moment later she pointed at a chocolate croissant. "I'll take that croissant, please!" she said happily.

The woman behind the counter looked at her. "I'm super sorry, the croissants have gluten in them..."

The woman in the queue shook her head. "That's fine! I'm not gluten intolerant."

Ricky looked on in disbelief. "This place is full of fuckin' lunatics," he thought to himself as he watched the lady take her croissant and leave the café.

"Hi there, what can I get for you?" said the woman behind the counter, smiling.

Ricky stumbled over his words. He had been so distracted by the circus act around him that he'd almost forgotten why he'd come.

"Hey, yeah, how's it goin'? I saw the sign out there sayin' that you were looking for staff and I figured I'd come and ask."

She eyed him up and down. "Oh, awesome! We're looking for a new kitchen hand – do you have much experience?"

"Yeah, loads, got heaps of experience!" lied Ricky. He'd never set foot in a professional kitchen in his life.

"That's great! Well, if you could just leave your name and number with me I'll tell the manager and she'll give you a call later today, ok?"

Ricky nodded and left his name and number on a napkin for her. "What was your name again, sorry?" he asked her.

"Samantha," she replied.

Ricky smiled. "No worries, well, thanks, Samantha, hopefully hear from ya soon."

He left the café easy as that and walked across the road to the pub opposite to wait for the call.

He sat at the pub a few hours. He didn't mind, he ordered a few schooners and got into conversation with an old boy who used to work underground in the mines.

The old boy's name was David, although he called himself Davo. Davo was in his late fifties, but he looked much older. When he mentioned he'd worked in the mines for thirty years, Ricky asked him what it was like. He knew a lot of people who'd gone to work in the mines, he'd even considered it himself. Everyone knew how much money there was to be made working there, but Ricky had never got around to going. Davo shook his head at the question before he told Ricky his story. "Seen a lot of awful things down in those mines. Takes a hold of you. Seen so many blokes move out to those mining towns with money in their eyes. Leave their missuses behind for a while, hopin' that they're gonna get enough to buy a nice house or somethin' later on and set a family up. Don't know what they're gettin' themselves into. Twelve-hour days of work, you start in the darkness of the early morning, and all day you're down in the dark, and by the time you finish work its fuckin' nighttime again. Eat, shit and sleep, that's all you fuckin' do out there besides work like a dog and breath in dust and grime and dirt all day. Worst bit was more than half of those blokes who came to save for a house got divorced, or their missus would cheat on them. Next thing they know their house is gone, and all that money they worked for and saved is split in half. Took me thirty years to save all my money, and then my wife left me and split it in two. Worst day of my life, signing the remaining workin' years of my life away to the mines just to get back to where I was before my missus left me..."

He shook his head again and drank from his beer. "Seen so many young blokes come there too, all eager to work and earn some coin. I wish they'd listen. There's better ways to earn money than that. Fuckin' dirt money, it is. You rock up to a beautiful landscape and within a couple months it's unrecognisable, raped and ruined by bulldozers and miners workin' all day and all night."

Ricky shook his head grimly, and the two drank to each other's sorrows.

It was four o'clock when Ricky's phone started buzzing in his pocket. He leant to one side on his bar stool and slipped it out of his pocket. "Ricky speakin'," he answered.

It was a woman's voice on the other end. "Hi Ricky, this is Emelia, I'm the manager at the Toast Café. I was just giving you a call to see if you'd be interested in coming in tomorrow morning for a trial shift? We'd have you down in the kitchen as kitchen hand, mainly washing dishes and doing food prep. How does that sound?"

"Yeh, sounds good! What time?" asked Ricky eagerly.

"Great, your shift would be from six in the morning till four in the afternoon," said Emelia.

"No worries, I'll see ya there!" said Ricky, before Emelia thanked him and hung up.

Ricky drove home excitedly; he felt as if a little weight had been lifted from his shoulders. The café was nowhere he would want to work for long, but at least it would bring in some money while he tried to figure something else out. He got home and cracked open a tinnie triumphantly before his phone buzzed again, but this time it was Emma.

She had sent a text message that read, "Come to the headland in twenty?"

He sighed and looked out of his window at the ocean.

Twenty minutes later he was trudging across the headland to the spot where he had first met

Emma a few days before. She was sitting there waiting for him, staring silently out towards the horizon.

"How ya goin'?" said Ricky as he approached her.

Her gaze shifted from the horizon to him, and she smiled warmly at him.

"Ricky! I'm good, and you?"

"Yeah, nah, I'm alright," he replied as he sat down next to her. "So, why'd you wanna meet up again?"

"I just had some questions," said Emma.

"Yeah?"

She paused for a moment before she asked, "What do you feel when you look out into the horizon?"

Ricky was taken aback. No one had ever asked him to express how he felt before, and he shied away from the question because it made him feel uncomfortable. But Emma waited patiently for a response, and after a few moments he gave up. "I dunno. Makes me feel good, I suppose."

Emma smiled at him, and he felt himself relax a little bit.

"But why does it make you feel good? I've been sitting here for a while now looking out into the horizon. It makes me feel small, but in a good way. I can see the birds flying past me and darting into the water for fish, and I can feel the balance in the world. It makes me feel like I'm a part of something way bigger than myself. But when I look at you I can tell that you see something completely different to me," she said.

"I dunno," he began. "It just makes me feel like myself."

"That's beautiful, Ricky," said Emma. "Have you been looking for a job?" she added.

"Yeah, actually, got a trial shift at some café in the city tomorrow mornin'!" said Ricky happily.

"That's great! I didn't take you for a barista."

"Nah, just doin' dishes and that, hopefully goes alright," he said.

"Have you ever thought of what you would do if you didn't have to work?" asked Emma. The sun was falling quickly and the bluish sky began to blend with a purple hue around them.

Ricky thought for a bit before he responded, "Nah, when I was a young bloke I always just imagined myself surfin' for my whole life, but now my knees are busted and my shoulders are so stiff I don't even reckon I could paddle, let alone stand."

"That's a shame," said Emma, "but at least you can still swim. You can still be in the water, and you can still feel like yourself when you're in it. That's a very special thing Ricky, I know a lot of people that would kill to be able to say that."

"Yeah, nah, you're right…" said Ricky. "What would you wanna do if you didn't work?" he asked Emma a moment later.

"Well… to tell you the truth, I've never really had to work…" she replied.

Hearing this astounded Ricky, who had started working when he was fourteen and never stopped. "Never had to work? Whaddya mean?"

Emma looked a little embarrassed. "Well, my grandad started a shipping container company decades ago and earned billions from it, and ever since that he's given all of us enough money to live on for the rest of our lives."

Ricky couldn't help himself. "Fuck me dead! What do you do all day then, if you don't work?"

"I'm an artist. I paint all day and listen to music. I spend all day mixing colours and splashing them in different ways to see how they'd come out, and then in the afternoons I swim and let the ocean wash the paint off of my body."

"Sounds nice, bein' an artist," said Ricky. "Sometimes when I look at nice views, or sunsets, they look like it's been painted, it's hard to believe sometimes."

"What do you mean?" asked Emma, prompting him to carry on.

"I dunno, like when you're lookin' at the sun setting over some mountains, and all the colours blend together and that. Just seems like it's meant to be, makes me feel like I'm a part of it all, makes me forget about stuff that's goin' on in my life for a moment."

"God! You see it now, don't you, Ricky? Not God as in the man in the sky, but God as in the everything. The thing that makes you feel like you're a part of it all. Because you are!" said Emma excitedly.

Ricky laughed. "Thought you weren't gonna talk about God anymore..."

Emma laughed, she'd been caught out.

"But nah, I kinda know what you're sayin' now," he followed up.

Emma grinned at him, and he smiled back. He didn't give a shit about God or anything, although he did understand what Emma was trying to tell him. He only cared about being with Emma. She was beautiful in every way, so much so that he could forgive her for trying to convert him to whatever she believed in.

Emma's phone started ringing, and when she answered it her smile faded.

"Sorry, Ricky, I've got to go. I'm meant to be taking my mum to the doctor's this afternoon."

"Nah, you're alright!" said Ricky. "Hope she's all good."

Emma smiled and thanked him, then they hugged and she left him sitting alone on the headland.

He sat there for a while, thinking about his own mum.

When he was a boy his mum was so strong and fierce. He both loved and respected her deeply because of the power she possessed within her. She would always drag him along to his nan's house to sit and watch soap operas with her, or those bad daytime gameshows. He'd always groan when she would force him to go, he'd have to sit there for hours whilst his nan kept explaining the shows to him. She'd point at the characters and say, "Oh, I like her, she's dating him, but she doesn't know that he's in love with her!"

When he was a little older she passed away, and all of a sudden, he felt regret and shame that he didn't go over to watch shows with her more. It made him sad inside to think that the only company she had were the characters in her shows, and not her grandson. He pictured her asleep, sitting on the sofa while the television still played in front of her, a small flashing beacon in a sea of darkness that consumed the lonely room.

And as time moved on and he got older he found himself in that room watching those same shows again, but this time it was his mum who explained them to him, and she'd point at her favourite characters and say, "I love him, he's so inappropriate! It's really a very silly show, isn't it?"

And although he tried to visit his mum as much as he could, he could never rid himself of the thought that when he was gone she was alone. Time moved on, and not long after his mum passed away too, and the room was empty, waiting patiently for the day when he took his seat on the sofa, and fell asleep while the television was on.

After that he constantly looked at himself in the mirror. He would look at the wrinkles around his eyes, or the sagging of his cheeks, and shiver. Long gone was the goofy kid that made everyone laugh with the faces he pulled. A part of him was happy that he'd never had a child. It would never have to see him grow old like his nan and his mum did.

The greatest realisation we can ever have in life is that one day we die, just like everyone else. It was the realisation Ricky was most proud of, because it reminded him that all things pass like grains of sand, or the pulling and pushing of the tide and swell.

5

The next day Ricky woke up early and got ready for his trial shift at the café. He chucked on an old shirt and some shorts and hopped in his van at half past five.

He was a little nervous; it'd been a long time since he'd had a first day at work, and he wasn't sure how he'd act, or what the people would be like. He figured he'd just focus on working hard, and the rest would come naturally.

When he arrived at the front door, Emelia the manager was waiting for him. She was young, in her early twenties, and trendy looking. Her hair was dyed purple, her nose and ears were pierced and she wore a pair of thick, heavy-looking leather boots.

Her smile was lovely.

"Morning! Are you Ricky?" she asked him.

"Mornin', yep, that's me," he replied.

"Cool, come on in. I'll show you around," she said as she led him through the door.

Ricky hadn't had a chance to look at the café properly the day before, he had been so distracted by all of the people that he hadn't bothered looking. It was a small and cosy place. The walls were half bare brick with wooden slats, and the floor was polished concrete. Emelia led him down some stairs to where the kitchen was.

In the kitchen there were two men: the chef, a tired-looking man in his late twenties, and his sous chef, a younger-looking guy with slicked-back hair. They both grunted when he came in.

"Boys, this is Ricky. He's doing a trial shift today for the kitchen hand position," said Emelia, and Ricky nodded at them.

They nodded back and Emelia left Ricky in the kitchen.

"You ever worked in a kitchen before, brother?" asked the chef.

Ricky shook his head.

"It's not fuckin' rocket science. Just stay at that sink and clean everything we pass to you as quick as you can. If I ask you to run into the cool room to grab me something you drop everything and get it."

"Sounds good," said Ricky. He went to the sink, which was already filled with that morning's prep utensils.

He grabbed the spray hose and scrubber and started cleaning. Once he was finished with the prep utensils he handed them to the chef, who examined them closely.

"The fuck is this?" he said. "Look at all that grime still in it... You gotta be more thorough than that."

He threw the freshly washed dishes back into the sink and Ricky started cleaning again.

"Better get a move on, service starts in fifteen minutes," added the chef.

Ricky cleaned the utensils just in time for service. After that, an endless stream of bowls, knives and forks flooded in, all of them covered in grime, egg and sauce. Ricky scrubbed as quickly as he could. He sprayed the hose so much that he became soaking wet, and as he rushed around the room he sweated and panted from the brutal work.

The chef yelled all day. Ricky had never heard someone swear so much, and he could have sworn that he'd seen the chef pull out a bag of cocaine and regularly take small bumps from it throughout the day.

At the end of service Ricky was exhausted, but he felt good. The kitchen was calm again, and as the two chefs washed down the benches and tidied up they talked and joked with Ricky.

Their names were Ed and Jimmy. Ed was the chef. He was a funny guy, but he was brutal too. Another guy was having a trial shift that day as a barista and he came down briefly to introduce himself to the chefs. He was young and handsome. There was something about his smugly attractive face that made Ricky want to punch him. He was talking to Ed when he said, "I'm actually a musician. I'm the lead singer and guitarist in a band."

He looked at Ed, waiting for praise, but Ed looked at him and said, "Oh yeah? That's weird – you look like a barista to me..."

Jimmy was a quiet guy, but he took Ed's shit well. He was able to dish out as many insults as Ed gave him, and Ed respected him for that. The two would constantly give each other shit all day, but it made the stressful service periods go quicker. Ricky had never seen two people work harder than them. For six hours straight they had their heads down, prepping, cooking and plating up food. The kitchen was hot while they worked, the grills bubbling and splashing boiling oil and the frying pans shooting up in flames as they cooked, and Ricky all of a sudden found a new respect for hospitality workers.

"You did good today, mate. I'll let them know and hopefully get you back down here with us," Ed said to Ricky once his shift had ended.

Ricky thanked him and said goodbye. He left the café, clothes soggy smelling horrible, but he felt happy about the day's work. He'd worked so hard he'd had no time to think. At the biscuit factory, he'd spend his days lost in thoughts and memories, feeling like he was slowly rotting away from the inside. But at the café he was so under the pump there was no time to think past what Ed was ordering him to do.

He drove straight to the beach, and when he dove into the water he felt the sweat and grime wash off his face and body and he smiled.

Half an hour later he was sitting on his sofa with a tinnie in hand when he got a call from Emma.

"How's it goin'?" he asked when he picked up the phone.

"Ricky! I'm good, how did your trial shift go?" she replied.

"Yeah, went good I reckon, hopefully got the job but will see I guess."

"That's good!" she said happlly. "I have a question for you."

"Yeah?" said Ricky.

"I think Byron Bay would be the perfect place to take you. I think the people there could show you how to get in tune with nature and manage your emotions better, what do you think?" she said.

"Byron? Isn't that the place that's full of fuckin' hippies?" said Ricky.

He heard Emma laugh. "No! Well, yes, actually, but you shouldn't be so dismissive of them. My father owns a property up there, it'd be free accommodation and free food. Besides, this could be your last chance to get away before you start working again. The beaches up there are beautiful..."

She made a strong argument. "Yeah, nah, sounds good, I'll go. When were you thinkin'?" asked Ricky.

"Tomorrow morning?"

"Yeah, alright, fuck it!" said Ricky.

"Awesome. I'll swing past your place around five in the morning and pick you up. It's a long drive."

"Sounds good, I'll see ya then," said Ricky, and Emma hung up.

He stood up from the sofa and packed some clothes into a rucksack. The more he thought about it, the more excited he got. It had been a long time since he'd left Sydney, and what was better was that he was going with Emma.

6

The next morning Emma arrived at Ricky's door at five o'clock. It was pitch black outside and all the stars were out as they drove. The first leg to Byron was a weird one. Sitting in a car with someone for the first time is always awkward – every silence was felt, and the pair both felt like each one needed to be filled with pointless questions. It took a few hours for them to be comfortable in silence together, and by that point the scenery had grown so wild and beautiful that they didn't need an excuse not to talk. They drove through mountains and rainforests, old farms that stretched out into the horizon, with rusty windmills standing lonely here and there. Ricky loved the countryside. He loved seeing remnants of old buildings and worn-out cars, they always stirred curiosity inside him.

Most of their conversations revolved around their families and childhoods. Emma had two siblings, a sister and a brother, but she was the youngest. Growing up she'd been given everything she'd ever wanted, but she'd always felt like there was something missing in her life. She felt disconnected from the real world, and that's when she turned to spirituality. In truth, she had much to learn about the real world, and that's why she wanted to be around Ricky. In a way, she needed to learn from him just as much as he needed to learn from her.

Ricky told her about his childhood. She loved listening to his stories; they were wildly different from her own. Her father was always restrictive with her, he'd never let her go to parties, or go off on her own. Ricky, on the other hand, lived his whole life outside. Jumping fences to get into parties he wasn't invited to, chasing girls, getting in fights and surfing big waves. He had more near-death stories than Emma had fingers to count. Most of them sounded like bullshit, but she made a game of trying to find the glimmers of truth in the tales.

The next day they arrived on the outskirts of Byron Bay. Emma took the wheel and drove towards somewhere where she told Ricky they could find a 'spiritual guru'.

Ricky couldn't help but roll his eyes. "Spiritual guru... I reckon we'll rock up to some skinny man wearing beads sittin' on top of some fuckin' waterfall or some shit. Then he'll spot us and pretend he knew we were comin' the whole time."

Emma was silent. Ricky was right about the beads and the waterfall bit. She'd been to Guru Naimki before. Years ago, when she first got into spiritualism, he guided her through her questions and showed her the answers that nature could provide. It was an incredibly memorable experience for her, and she was hoping that Guru Naimki could do the same for Ricky too.

They pulled up out front of an old rusty gate that had a wooden sign attached to it reading 'Peace and Love to all who enter'.

Beyond the gate was a rocky dirt road that disappeared into a lush rainforest. It looked beautiful, and as they drove up slowly they soaked in as much of their surroundings as possible.

At the end of the road there was an old but elegant house made of wood. There were wind chimes and crystals all around that gave the place a feeling of zen.

"Come on," said Emma quietly, "I think he's by the waterfall."

Ricky laughed. "Fuckin' told ya so!"

It wasn't exactly a waterfall, more of a small stream that trickled down some mossy rocks, but the forest was so quiet all they could hear was the peaceful trickle and gurgle of the water.

Guru Naimki was sitting by it in the middle of a deep meditation, but he opened his eyes when the pair approached him and smiled.

"Emma!" he said, standing up and raising his arms.

They embraced and Emma turned to Ricky. "This is my friend Ricky. I was hoping that you'd be able to guide him through some of his questions."

He smiled again. "Of course." He raised his arms and walked over to Ricky to embrace him.

Ricky stuck out his hand awkwardly. "Put it there, mate." He felt like he'd put himself out there enough as it was, without having to hug some hippy in the middle of a forest.

Guru Naimki understood. He'd had a lot of Ricky's types come through for his teachings. They were hard work, but most of them came around at least in some way in the end.

"Come on, let's go have a tea back at the house," suggested Naimki.

The interior of the old wooden shack was beautiful and elegant. Aside from being a guru, Naimki was also an artist, and his art was strung up on every wall. It was mostly abstract paintings, with colours and shades splashed and mixed around the canvas, but Ricky spotted a detailed drawing of a tree that he liked the look of.

"Some nice artwork you got here, boss," said Ricky.

"Thanks. It's not hard to find the inspiration around here," said Naimki as he put the kettle on and prepared the tea.

With the drinks prepared, Naimki took a seat and asked, "So, Ricky, what are these questions?"

Ricky didn't know what to say. He'd never felt like he had any questions, he just knew he felt stuck. "I dunno, I guess it's just about everything," he said after a moment.

Naimki laughed. "That's a big question, and unfortunately one I don't have the answer to."

"Well, what am I doin' here, then? I thought you'd have some kind of powers or something," joked Ricky cheekily.

"The only power I have is being able to brew a good tea, and that's good enough for me," said Naimki.

Emma sat back silently. She knew how Naimki worked; he was a genius. In a past life Naimki had been a leading psychologist. He grew up in Sydney but he had studied overseas in the United Kingdom. He loved his job, but after a while he became disillusioned with modern life. He had a lot of problems, but mostly he was lonely. He loved too much, is what he used to say to himself. He loved to the point where he loved other people more than he loved himself. That hurt him. He couldn't engage in any relationships without feeling vertigo, and in the ceaseless erratic movements of the city he often felt like a shell of a man, walking around without any purpose in his life. He used to watch the world go by as he rode the bus to work, and he'd get little glimpses of people's lives on his commute. People unloading things out of their cars, people jogging together or sitting alone on park benches. Like Ricky, he felt like there were only a few types of people you could become, and somehow, everybody became one of them. That thought scared him; he was scared of becoming conditioned to and moulded into that person by the ceaseless grind of inner city life. That's when he moved to the outskirts of Byron Bay. He'd always been interested in spirituality, and as a psychologist he was curious and respectful of how it helped people reach an equilibrium in their lives.

"Let's start with this. How do you cope when you have a bunch of questions that you can't seem to get an answer to?" asked Naimki, pouring the tea.

"I dunno, I don't really. I just let it stew, I guess. Or I drink it out with the boys, we have a laugh and it all feels ok again for a little while," said Ricky.

Naimki nodded his head and sipped from his tea. "In reality, Ricky, I don't have any answers to your questions. One day you will find them within yourself if you look hard enough. What I can show you is how to manage the emotions that circle around such big questions. Not knowing is scary – it can make you frustrated and lonely, and those are two deep emotions that can easily trickle into other parts of your life. The easiest way to get rid of these emotions is to practice thankfulness for what you do have in your life. Praise be! That's all there is to it. You'd be surprised by how much weight you keep buried within yourself. When you're thankful you're releasing the bad weight from your soul, and offering it up to the universe to heal. The trees, the birds, the sea...they are all as much of you as your hands and feet. If you give thanks, even the stormiest days can offer hope and warmth. There are times I wake up feeling sorry for myself, but as soon as I say 'Praise be' and give thanks to the universe my mindset changes completely! Try it yourself. Think of something, any of your questions, and without worrying yourself too much with them simply say, 'Praise be'."

All of a sudden Ricky became shy – he didn't like the idea of proclaiming praise to the universe like that himself. It made him feel uncomfortable.

Naimki realised this and turned to Emma. "You know this well, Emma. Come on, on the count of three let's all say 'Praise be!'"

Emma nodded, and on the count of three she and Naimki exclaimed in unison, "Praise be!"

Ricky mouthed the words, hoping he'd get away with it, but Naimki was watching him and he shook his head. "Come on, Ricky! What do you have to be scared of?"

"I'm not scared..." said Ricky defensively.

"Then join in with us!" smiled Emma excitedly.

Ricky couldn't refuse Emma, and on three they all said, "Praise be!"

He couldn't tell if it was because he didn't have to say it anymore, or because it really had an effect, but after giving thanks he did feel a little lighter.

"Yeah, you're right, that does feel a bit better," said Ricky, and Naimki smiled.

"I'm glad," said Naimki, and a moment later he stood up and lifted something from the kitchen shelf.

"Have you ever seen one of these before?" he asked Ricky as he brought the object over and sat back down. In his other hand, he was holding a large brass-looking bowl with a pestle.

"This is a singing bowl," said Naimki, and he began to circle the pestle on the edge of the bowl. He ran it softly around the rim, around and around until Ricky could hear a faint humming, and as Naimki circled it grew louder, to the point where Ricky could not just hear it, but feel its vibrations in the air. As it rang through his body in waves he closed his eyes.

A moment later he opened them again, scared to death of the emotions that had suddenly crept their way to the surface.

"Fuck me dead, could ya stop playing that thing?" he said, trying to keep composed. He never realised just how many emotions he had buried deep down inside himself.

Naimki instantly stopped playing and looked at him. "Is everything ok, Ricky?"

Ricky nodded, "Yeah, jus' not in the mood for that thing."

"That's ok, the singing bowl isn't for everyone. I've got one more exercise for today for you to take with you." Naimki stood up, walked back over to the shelf and picked up a long, thin packet. He opened it and pulled out two brown sticks that Ricky instantly recognised as incense. He'd seen them in all the Thai massage places he'd ever gone to, and he smirked cheekily.

Naimki lit the incense sticks and invited Ricky to sit on his knees by them.

"You may find this next exercise hard – most people do," said Naimki. He disappeared into the next room and returned holding a full-sized mirror. He placed it in front of Ricky.

Ricky looked at himself in the mirror and laughed; it was an awkward thing to do in front of other people.

Naimki stood next to him. "I want you to look at yourself in the eyes. Stay quiet and still the whole time, and try not to get distracted."

"Sounds simple enough," said Ricky.

Naimki turned on a pair of speakers that sat on his kitchen bench, and played a soundtrack of deep meditation music.

Ricky looked at himself in the eyes. At first, he was trying not to laugh – the whole situation felt completely ridiculous to him – but after thirty seconds he was struggling not to cry. He didn't know why, he just hated looking at himself. There was something in his eyes that he'd always known was there, but as the years passed he'd ignored it more and more. It was the glimmer of purity within himself that he used to cherish growing up. When he was a boy he swore to himself that he'd never grow up, and if he ever did he would never lose touch with his childhood self. He made that pact the night before his thirteenth birthday, but he never kept his end of the bargain. He hated seeing that glimmer of his childhood self – it reminded him of just how far he was away from the person he thought he'd become.

Suddenly he grew irritated, what could a couple of incense sticks and a relaxing song do against a whole lifetime of bitterness and disappointment? He turned his head away from the mirror and tried to swallow the lump in his throat.

"You did well, Ricky. That's never an easy exercise, but it's one that's necessary in growing and discovering the questions you have deep inside of yourself," said Naimki, before turning the music off.

"Yeah... I see what you mean."

Naimki stood. "I think that's enough for now. If ever you want to come back, Ricky, please feel free to do so. It'll take a lot more than just one session for you to grow to your full potential, but I hope you can at least take one lesson from today."

"Praise be?" asked Ricky.

Naimki nodded. "Praise be…"

Emma stood up, smiling at Ricky. She looked very proud of him. "Thank you, Guru Naimki."

The pair hugged goodbye, then she and Ricky left, hopping back in Emma's car and driving towards Byron.

"So, what did you think of that?" asked Emma.

Ricky shrugged. "Yeah, was alright I spose," he said, trying to play the experience down, even though he and Emma both knew that it had affected him.

"It's always hard the first time, but Guru Naimki is right. Giving praise is the best way to feel connected with the universe, with God."

"Yeah, I'm gonna try doin' it for sure," said Ricky, although he knew himself too well. The Ricky he knew would do it one morning and then give up the next.

Twenty more minutes of driving passed before they finally reached Byron. The road down was beautiful; it wound and turned, and all around was dense jungle.

Ricky was excited to see Byron Bay for himself. He'd heard a lot of different things about it and he wanted to make a judgement for himself. Once they finally made it into town, Ricky tried to absorb as much as he could as they drove through. It wasn't what he expected, to say the least. Ricky had always imagined Byron to be a quiet, tranquil place filled with hippies that walked with no shoes on and smoked weed all day. He saw those kinds of people, but they were drowned out by a sea of tourists that assailed the colourful shops. The pavement was crowded with people, and they all bustled past one another impatiently. It reminded him of Sydney.

Emma was trying in vain to find a parking spot, but everywhere was full, not to mention the prices for parking were almost extortionate.

By the time they found somewhere and started walking Ricky was in a foul mood.

"What the fuck is this?" asked Ricky, looking around almost in disgust.

Emma sighed, "Byron's not quite what it used to be, but you can still find its soul if you look hard enough."

"Fuck me dead, you'd need a fuckin' microscope to find the soul in this place," said Ricky.

Ricky hated Byron Bay. It didn't take him long. He looked around at all of the hip people and it made him furious. To him, it looked like everyone was pretending to be from there, and none of them realised that nobody was. Decades ago, real hippies had moved up to Byron and made it their own. There were radical thinkers, drug takers and travellers all in the one place, creating an interesting town built around renewable living and an ecology with nature and the natural spirit. But, as the years passed, word got out about Byron, and people from all over Australia and eventually all over the world came to visit it. Years of tourism took their toll and the spirit of Byron had been whitewashed by the very same capitalism that the originators had sought to escape. Now Byron was just a place where dreams were sold. The surfer's dream, the hippie's dream, and the stoner's dream were all marketed and sold at a profit, and the spirit of Byron was sold along with it. It made Ricky feel silly about buying into Guru Naimki. He felt just as much of a fool as the tourists that crowded around the tie-dye shirt shops, throwing money at whatever souvenirs they could get their hands on.

Suddenly he felt angry at being brought to Naimki, and made to sit through the meditation and the singing bowl.

"This place is full of fuckin' posers!" said Ricky.

"Ricky! You can't say that, you're just looking at it from the surface level," said Emma, looking over her shoulder to make sure no one heard.

"Nah, fuck this – all I see is a bunch of cunts pretending to be something they're not!"

"Ricky, seriously, if you don't shut up then we'll go home," said Emma sternly.

A skinny man with dreadlocks and no shoes on approached the pair with a look of concern on his face. He looked at Emma, at her beautiful bronze skin and flowing floral dress, and then to Ricky, who was wearing denim jeans, a button-up plaid shirt, and a rugby league cap, and figured something was wrong about the pair.

"Excuse me, is he bothering you?" said the man, pointing at Ricky.

Ricky had had enough. He'd been dragged along all day, made to smell incense, listen to singing bowls and meditate, and now some skinny hippie was arking up at him." Ah, get fucked, dog," he spat at the man.

The man pushed Ricky. "Get the fuck away from her, you fucking square!"

Emma tried to get between the two, desperately trying to defuse the situation, but Ricky was beyond the tipping point.

"What are ya gonna do? Hit me? You'd fuckin 'break your brittle little arms, you malnourished cunt!"

A moment later, Ricky was lying on his back, dazed and confused after being king hit by the man with dreadlocks.

Emma gasped, "Ricky!" and tried to lift him, but his legs were like jelly.

The man and his friends ran off, and Ricky sat there on the pavement for a while trying to recoup. He looked at Emma, a stream of blood gushing from his bottom lip, and laughed." Fuck this place..."

Seeing Ricky laugh made Emma laugh too. "Well, I guess you asked for it."

"Yeah, nah... I had that one comin', didn't I?" said Ricky as he collected himself enough to stand slowly.

"Come on, let's go back..." said Emma, turning to leave.

Ricky stopped her and smiled. "Nah, it's all good, let's keep goin'. I've learned my lesson."

7

For the rest of the afternoon, Emma and Ricky walked around Byron listening to the music, trying the food and watching the people. Ricky grew used to it after a while, and by the end of the day he didn't mind it so much.

As the day came to a close Emma and Ricky drove to Emma's property just outside of Byron. It was a small, cute-looking cottage that sat above a rocky hill.

It was a nice place, one that made Ricky think it'd be nice to move out to the countryside when he got a little older. He'd always figured he was a country boy. Even though he loved the ocean, he hated the city. Sometimes he felt claustrophobic walking down the street. People walked at different paces: some people walked so fast they were basically stepping on your heels, others walked too slowly and zigzagged aimlessly so that he was forced to sidestep and rush past them. There was too much going on at once, and he felt like there was no reason for any of it.

Emma showed him to his room and he dropped his bags and had a shower before coming out into the living room again to find her pouring wine into two glasses.

"Maybe tonight's the night I get a root," he joked to himself.

"Do you want the good news or the bad news?" said Emma as Ricky took a seat at the kitchen table.

"Good news, I reckon..." Ricky replied.

"The good news is that we have wine. The bad news is there's no food in the house. After the day we've had, I completely forgot to go shopping!"

"Nah, that's alright, I couldn't be fucked to cook anyways. Any takeout places round this area?"

"We should go for Chinese!" said Emma.

"Chinese?" Ricky had never been to a Chinese restaurant in his life, but he'd opened up a little bit to the idea of trying new things after his day in Byron so he agreed.

Later that evening, Emma brought him to the Golden Dragon, a local Chinese restaurant down the road from her place.

They took a seat and looked at the menu. Ricky couldn't see a single thing he'd want to eat, so Emma ordered for him. She asked for a plate of lemon chicken, some dumplings and some fried duck.

Ricky picked up his chopsticks and eyed them with a wry smile. "What've they gone and given me a pair of drumsticks for?"

"Ricky! You can't say that, it's disrespectful," said Emma in a hushed voice.

Ricky winked at her and grinned, sometimes he loved making Emma feel just as uncomfortable as she made him. He meant no disrespect, but he was brought up on a piss-take culture. To him, it was funny to take the piss out of things, and he'd laugh just as hard if someone were to take the piss out of him too.

Twenty minutes passed before the food came out, and when it did Ricky's eyes lit up. "Fuck me dead, this looks pretty good!"

"What did I tell you?" laughed Emma. She was enjoying watching Ricky experience new things. She'd grown up lucky enough to come from a cultured family. Growing up, she'd always go on holidays overseas, they'd eat the food, experience the culture and talk to the people, and as a result she was open and willing to immerse herself into different experiences.

When her food came out she slurped it with her chopsticks in hand and Ricky looked at her in disgust.

"What the fuck are you slurpin' like that for?" he said.

"It's how you eat in China – it lets them know that you think the food is good."

Ricky shook his head in disbelief. "It's like it's fuckin' Opposite Day in here or something. You eat with sticks, slurp the food – what? When we leave do we tell the waiter to get fucked too?"

Emma laughed. She knew Ricky well enough at this point to realise when he was blatantly trying to get a reaction out of her.

Ricky stopped talking once he tried the food. He ate it with gusto, and even slurped a bit too to keep Emma happy. He loved it. He loved the entire aesthetic of the restaurant too, the fact that it was family owned and operated, and that other Chinese families were in there having dinner and talking amongst themselves. It was one big community, and Ricky respected that.

Later that night they were back at Emma's house drinking wine and listening to music, and Emma was midway through telling him the story of how she came to meet Guru Naimki.

"When I was younger I ran away from home. I was so confused about everything in my life, and I just needed space. I felt guilty about it for so long, I left right after my dad and I had a big argument, and he worried about me for weeks because he thought he'd never see me again. I was fine, I hopped on a train to Byron because I knew a bunch of my friends had gone there and said it was the best time of their lives.

"When I got to Byron it was different than it is now. It was grungy and raw; there were so many vagrants and travellers from all around the world there. I had money saved from what my granddad gave me for my birthday, so I stayed in one of the hostels for some time. That's where I met Guru Naimki. He was showing a group of backpackers how to meditate in the courtyard, and he asked me if I wanted to try it too. I remember when I first closed my eyes I felt ridiculous, but after a few minutes I started focusing on myself and everything that was causing me problems in my life. I didn't really find an answer, but I found specific problems, and I guess that was a start. When I left he told me that if I ever wanted to learn more from him I was always welcome to visit him at his place, and so I did!"

Ricky felt a hint of jealousy at the way Emma talked about Naimki, and he secretly hoped to himself that their relationship was never anything more than just meditation.

But what would it matter anyway? he thought to himself. He was years older than her, and he felt undeserving of her grace and her beauty.

"What problems could you have had? You're a fuckin' beautiful young woman, and you're smart and humble too. I've met a lot of lasses in my life, but you've got to be my favourite," said Ricky. He was drunk on the red wine, but he meant what he said. He'd thought a lot about his relationship with Eliza since meeting Emma. He was so young when they met, they were both young. She was his first love, but it was a love that he never understood properly until now. He loved Eliza out of the fear of losing her. Their love was one that made him self-conscious and capricious of himself, and she was always highlighting his short-comings. Emma was nothing but open and supportive. She accepted him for who he was, and he respected her deeply for her outlook on life.

Emma blushed a little. "Well, thanks, Ricky. But my point is, on the headland that day I saw a bit of me in you. You seemed lost and confused, but there's a light in your eyes that I know searches for more, and I can feel that in your very being. You try hard to give off a rough persona, Ricky, but I'm not convinced that that's you at all."

"Yeah – you might be right, I dunno. I never used to be a rough bloke. When I was a kid I was soft and playful, I used to go out and explore every day and play games with my friends and that. I never wanted to grow up, now I think about it. Fuck me, I remember the night before my thirteenth birthday I was devastated, I was layin' in bed all sad 'cus I thought the next day I'd have to stop bein' a kid. I loved bein' a kid. So, I made a promise to myself that I'd never let go of my childhood. Guess I broke that promise a while back..."

"What were your teenage years like?" asked Emma. She realised she was finally about to see Ricky open up to her, and it wasn't an opportunity that she was going to miss.

"Yeah, they were good too. Just surfed and that, chased girls, partied and all the usual stuff. I lost a lot of friends, though. My mum sent me to a private school for a bit, but I fuckin' hated it. Full of try-hards and self-proclaimed people. I remember after I left that school I ran into a couple of the boys from there and they were on about how they were this and that. If there's one thing I've learned in life, it's that self-proclaimed people are full of shit, they want you to think they're somethin' so bad that they'll make the judgement for you and try and force it into your head. I couldn't stand it. When I was seventeen or somethin' I used to love English. I loved stories as a kid. I dunno, I still do, I guess, but I just never read any. But all the boys in my English class used to idolize this bloke called Oscar Wilde, I dunno if you know him?"

Emma smiled, "I've heard of him, of course!" She was surprised that Ricky knew him too.

Ricky nodded. "Well, he's meant to be known for bein' all witty and that, which he was. I remember reading some of his shit when I was younger and it would blow my mind. But the boys in my class fuckin' ruined the whole experience for me. They loved Oscar Wilde so much they all tried to act like him. Only problem was that Oscar Wilde was a literary genius, these boys were just stuck-up cunts!

"Haven't picked up a book since those days. I knew from then on that I didn't wanna be anything like those boys at that private school. I wanted to be a man's man."

"What do you mean by that?" Emma asked.

"I don't even know anymore…" said Ricky. "Haven't felt like a man's man in a long time, not since my missus left me. A man's man wouldn't fuckin' run away from his problems like I did…"

"You put a lot of pressure on yourself, Ricky, you're only human," said Emma empathetically. She put her hand on his shoulder and Ricky felt its warmth and smiled.

"Yeah, I guess so. That was one of the biggest realisations I had after my divorce. I'm just like every other bloke that swings down to the pub every arvo and pisses away his paycheque. I dunno, when you're younger and that you reckon the whole world's lookin' at you."

"You're not like those guys at all!" said Emma, but before she could continue Ricky cut her off. He felt like he'd come across wrong – the truth was he loved that realisation.

"Nah, nah, it's a good thing. I used to put way more pressure on myself 'cus I reckoned I was special. I always thought I'd grow up to be someone, if that even means anything. That was one of the best days of my life when I realised I was just like every other cunt, 'cus I stopped caring what people thought of me. I realised it didn't even matter in the end."

Emma had never thought of it like that. She had always been of the opinion that everyone was special in their own little ways, but she could see where Ricky was coming from, even though she didn't agree with him.

"I know what you mean, but you are special, Ricky. If not to the world then you are to me," she said, smiling.

Ricky felt warm all over. It was nice to hear Emma say something like that; it did make him feel special in a way.

"I guess that's what families and friends and loved ones are for. At least you can be special and unique to them. My granddad was a special one. He used to get super pissed up on a Sunday afternoon, and when I'd come round with my mum he'd always pull his teeth out and try and gross me out with them, or he'd sit me down and tell me some stories from way back when him and his friends used to surf on old boards and that."

"Surfing is really a big part of your life, isn't it?" said Emma.

"Yeah… it was my world until I fucked my knees up. There's nothin' like it. When the waves are big and you're feelin' kinda scared, and you start paddling for one your heart starts racin' a million miles an hour, and when you stand and take the drop you feel butterflies in your stomach. But nothin' beats the feeling of getting barrelled. When you take a steep drop and pull into a barrel you can feel the full force of the wave, and you hear it crashing and exploding all around you. It's like you're racin' through a tight little tunnel that's collapsing in front of you."

"That sounds amazing, Ricky. I wish I could share that experience with you," said Emma.

"I'll teach ya one time!" Ricky replied excitedly. "I got a bunch of boards that'd be perfect for you to learn on. I'll take you down when it's small and calm and I can just push you onto the waves to start, until you can paddle for them on your own."

"That sounds nice," said Emma, warmly.

The two of them became silent. They were sitting next to one another now as they drank, and a strange tension began to grow between the two.

If Ricky were drunker he would have leaned in and gone for a kiss at that moment. He felt like there was something in the air that hadn't been there before they started talking, but he couldn't tell if it was because he was drunk, so he thought it best to not act on it.

There was something in the air, and Emma felt it too. Even though he was years older than she was, she took pride in watching him grow and come out of his shell, even more so because it was a result of her actions. It felt empowering to her almost, to watch him open up and smile like that. She could see his face light up as he pictured and described his memories, reminiscing on better times. That night she saw a glimpse of who Ricky truly was. He was energetic and passionate and opinionated; he had just chosen a path through life that subdued those things in him. It was a life spent working hard and earning nothing. Those happy emotions were much like muscle memory, and she hoped that as he reminisced on them, a little of their essence and purity would rub off on him again. More and more she felt herself becoming drawn to him – his life was a life so unlike hers, and the great unknown of the working world intrigued her deeply. The more time she spent with Ricky the more she picked up on his little nuances. He swore too much, but he was almost always softly spoken, and there was something poetic about the way he looked at things, through eyes that had experienced too much disappointment, and too little love.

She almost felt like it was her duty to love him, because it seemed as if no one else had. She didn't care about looks or age – maybe when she was younger she had – but after her journey into spiritualism those things were just as superficial as the clothes on his back. But she was just as drunk as Ricky, and figured getting any closer physically would just make things awkward.

"Let's surf tomorrow!" said Ricky, breaking the silence. His knees weren't what they used to be when he was younger, but he'd cop the pain just to show Emma that he could still surf. He couldn't pretend that thought of seeing her in a bikini may have had something to do with his eagerness to teach her as well.

Emma laughed, "No way! I'd be so bad, it'll be super embarrassing…"

Ricky waved her off, "Nah you'll be right! Trust me…"

Emma couldn't turn him down, she'd never seen him so excited to do something. She realised it was because he was always putting himself out there to do something with her, and that made her feel better about giving surfing a go.

8

The next morning Ricky rushed off to rent some boards from one of the local surf shops, and he met Emma at the beach carpark. It was a sunny day without much wind, and the waves were small and gentle. They rolled slowly to the shore leaving a trail of white wash bubbling lazily behind them.

Ricky pulled up next to her carrying two large old looking foam boards under his arm. He took one look at the surf and grinned, "Fark, day for it!"

Emma smiled at him, it made her happy seeing him so excited. It was like she was with someone entirely different to the Ricky she knew. His eyes were lit up with a fire she'd not seen in them before, and as they put on their sunscreen and made their way down to the water Ricky almost power walked in front of her.

Ricky went first, he dove headfirst into the water, and when he came out again he beamed at her. It was like the Ricky that worked at the biscuit factory and felt bitter towards everything had been washed away by the water, instead replaced by a youthful looking man with wells of happiness and understanding in his eyes.

"Come in the waters super nice!" he called out to her.

Emma was standing ankle deep, holding her waterlogged foam surfboard awkwardly with two hands on her side. The waves had looked gentle and small at the carpark, but now that she was up close to them she felt terrified to get into the water. But Ricky outstretched his hands to her, and she forgot about the waves and hopped in.

The water was warm and smooth feeling. Emma struggled onto her board and tried to paddle. It was much harder than she was expecting, but Ricky paddled alongside her, and every time a wave would come their way he'd guide her through. She learned that when you're on a big board you need to roll upside down when a wave comes so it washes over you, instead of pushing you back to shore.

When they finally made it out the back Emma was exhausted. She lay on her board with her head resting on her arms and watched Ricky turn around and paddle for a wave. It amazed her how he knew when and where to paddle, he made it look like second nature as he stood up, and a moment later he was gliding gently across the wave. He whooped in delight as he passed her. Ricky hadn't surfed for a very long time, and even though his knees felt stiff and painful, he knew it was worth it. He was laughing when he paddled back up to Emma, "still got it aye!"

This is where Ricky truly belonged, Emma thought to herself as she watched him. He'd already caught three waves in the first five minutes they'd paddled out, and every time he hopped off one, she saw him paddling back out eagerly for more.

Suddenly a wave was forming right in front of where Emma was laying on her board. Her heart started pounding, and even though it was a small wave, it felt like a mountain to her.

Ricky paddled as fast as he could towards her, he was egging her on to paddle for it. He knew she wouldn't go for it, and just before the wave reached her Ricky managed to push her board forwards with enough momentum that the wave carried her with it. Emma gripped the board as tight as she could and closed her eyes, and as she felt herself drop down the wave she screamed. White wash exploded all around her and she bobbed this way and that. It was an exhilarating feeling, and even though she hadn't even tried to stand up she could hear Ricky cheering behind her.

"That was great!" she said excitedly to Ricky when he paddled over to help her get back past the waves again.

Ricky couldn't stop smiling at her, and every time he laughed she could hear so much joy in it.

"Ricky this is amazing..." she said to him after they'd been sat out the back for a while. She'd lost herself in the horizon, and every now and then she'd lay with her back on her board and look up at the clouds passing lazily above.

"Yeah..." said Ricky, he was looking out at the horizon too.

Emma looked at Ricky differently after that. She'd finally seen what she knew was inside of him all along. He was beautiful, and full of joy, it'd just been stifled by the hole he'd got himself caught up in.

"You shoulda seen me back in the day," began Ricky, the two of them were sitting on the beach watching the waves after they hopped out of the water, "I used to be able to surf so much better. I could do a coupla good airs, and if it was barrelling I was more than likely gonna come out of a couple."

"It's amazing Ricky. I feel so silly that I've never tried to surf before, even though I've lived next to the beach my entire life..."

Ricky smiled at her, "Nah don't feel silly, it's always better when you're doin' it with someone else."

Ricky started surfing when he was nine years old. He started because he saw the older boys in his area doing it, and all he wanted to be at the time was like them. He begged his mum for a board for months, but she refused to buy him one. Ricky hated her for it. It wasn't until he was older that he realised it wasn't because she didn't want him to start surfing, it was because she couldn't afford to buy him a board. In her head, she decided that she'd rather him think her too strict of a mother than too poor. She was embarrassed, and it made her feel like she couldn't provide for her son, and that made her angry. She was as fierce and loving as a mother could be, and Ricky was grateful every day that he was her son. The day we grow up is the day we begin to feel ashamed about the grievances we caused in our youths. Ignorant and blind to the struggles that people face behind closed doors, cocky and delusional in our assumptions, but that is the place of youths. They hold us accountable for the great debt we owe to our own creation and upbringing. All that life is, is in you, and all that you see is yourself.

On his ninth birthday Ricky opened up his bedroom door to find an old, beaten up looking surfboard waiting for him in the hallway. He couldn't believe his eyes. He picked it up in his hands and held it in front of himself, he felt the fibre glass and smelled the old wax, he caressed the rails of the board and looked up at its nose, studying every inch of its beaten deck.

He rushed into his mum's room and hugged her so hard that all she could do was laugh and pat him gently on the head. She'd worked overtime for three weeks straight so that she could buy him a board for his birthday. She'd managed to save a few hundred dollars, but when she arrived at the surfboard shop she almost fainted at the price of a brand-new surfboard. Macca, the shop owner saw her, and when she explained her story to him he was so moved that he gave her one of his old boards for free. She couldn't believe his generosity, although he felt as if it was the least he could do- it was an old board and he hadn't surfed it in years, but he was happy that it could find a new home with Ricky.

That afternoon she drove Ricky down to the beach and watched him surf. He rushed out into the water and came back ten minutes later spluttering and out of breath. He'd paddled straight into the impact zone and a couple of waves rattled him around so badly that he had to turn around and go back in. She was worried that Ricky would quit before he even started, but he went every single morning and afternoon after that day. Before school and after school he was surfing. He'd wake up in the dark and paddle out as the sun rose, and when the sun set he'd watch the golden light set the clouds ablaze, and afterwards he'd look up at the stars and the moon.

"Thank you, Ricky." Said Emma after a long silence.

Ricky smiled but he didn't reply, his heart told him that he was better off not saying anything at all.

9

The next morning they drove home, and as Ricky looked out over the disappearing countryside he replayed the previous few days over and over in his head. He was certain there was something between them, and as he thought about the connection he felt with Emma he tried to suppress a smile. Emma noticed the look on his face, however, and asked, "What are you smiling for?"

"Ah, nothin', was just daydreamin' about a funny memory," he replied.

That evening they pulled up to Ricky's place after a long day of driving.

Ricky was exhausted, but in good spirits as he unbuckled his seatbelt. "Thanks for makin' me come up there with you. I really appreciate it."

Emma smiled. "Of course! I'm relieved you enjoyed it, a part of me was worried that you wouldn't."

"Nah, I would have enjoyed it no matter what we were gonna do. I like spendin' time with you, it makes me feel at ease," said Ricky, and Emma almost blushed.

"The same to you, Ricky. I feel like I've learned just as much as you have," said Emma.

Ricky left the car, but before he turned to go into the house, Emma got out and hugged him goodbye.

It was different from any of the friendly hugs she'd given him before; it seemed a lot more intimate, and it lasted for a second longer than usual.

The next day Ricky woke up early and headed straight to the headland. He wanted to try giving thanks, and figured that the headland spot would be a good place to start. It was a clear morning and the sun was only just above the edge of the horizon when he arrived. The few clouds in the sky were stained with pinkish-red light, and a soft, cool breeze blew gently by.

"Fuck me, I'm pretty lucky, aren't I?" Ricky said to himself as he took a seat.

He sat there silently for a while, taking it all in, before breathing in deeply and saying, "Praise be."

He felt good to appreciate it all. He had always appreciated his home, but he'd never put it into a phrase, and the action seemed to stir a feeling of positive energy inside of him.

He felt lighter when he left the headland, lifted by the breeze and the sun and the salt in the air.

His day would only improve from there. A few hours later he got a call from the café telling him he'd got the job and that his first shift would be on the following Monday.

He was ecstatic, and once he hung up he sent Emma a message straight away which read, 'Got the job!'

She sent him a text message back a moment later, which read, 'Yay! :)'

Things seemed to be going ok for him, and he noticed that for the first time in years he was actually looking forward to the future. He didn't feel as if he was just floating from one sting to the next, and what was better was that he had a friend to share it with.

He was thankful for the ocean, and the sun and the wind, but most of all he was thankful for Emma. In just a short time she had already brought so much balance into his world, and he felt in debt to her kindness.

He didn't go to the pub that night. Instead he called Emma up and asked her if she wanted to go out for dinner. He wanted to take her out somewhere nice to thank her for the trip to Byron, but he also wanted to tell her how he felt about her. He couldn't stop thinking about his feelings for her. When he was trying to sleep, when he got up in the morning, when he was brushing his teeth or at the supermarket, he was constantly thinking of Emma. Even if she did end up rejecting him, at least he would have an answer. He gulped at the idea of being rejected by her. He knew she would shut him down softly if she did, and that almost made it worse.

He would take disgust over pity any day. At least if she was repulsed by the idea then he could walk away feeling like a man. If she let him down softly he'd feel like a boy asking out an older girl and her feeling too guilty to laugh at him.

He met her at a quarter to seven at a local Italian restaurant. It wasn't exactly fine dining, but the atmosphere was comfortable and the food that came out was hearty and wholesome. Emma looked even more beautiful than usual, and as they ate she congratulated him on getting the job at the café.

"That's so amazing, Ricky! At least you'll have some money coming in while you look for a more permanent job."

"Yeah... exactly. I didn't mind the work there to be honest either. Was hard work but the time went quick and the boys in the kitchen were alright."

"Who knows, maybe you'll become a chef!" said Emma.

"Yeah, get me on the chicken straight up, I'll give everyone in a ten-kilometre radius food poisoning..."

They laughed, and a moment later the waiter arrived with two plates, one with bolognese and the other lasagne. The waiter put the plates down and Emma and Ricky halved them between each other. Emma didn't even get halfway through eating her first section of bolognese before she gave up, so Ricky finished off her food for her too.

"Fuck, I'm stuffed," said Ricky, with his hands on his stomach.

A moment later he regretted it, though. He realised he'd probably just made himself look like a massive slob, but if Emma cared at all she didn't show it.

"Me too! That was so nice, thanks for bringing me here, Ricky," she said.

With the end of the night steadily approaching, Ricky's heart started racing. He'd been trying to avoid bringing up the burning conversation for the entire dinner, but now it was coming to an end he felt it was now or never to tell her how he felt about her.

"Nah, of course! Thank you for takin' me up to Byron. Honestly, the dinner was the least I could do." He paused for a moment with a lump in his throat, hung up on the next words. "I, ah, wanted to talk to you about somethin' too."

Emma picked up on his hesitation and leant in curiously. "Sure, what's up?"

He couldn't do it. He'd never been so scared in his life and all of a sudden it felt like the entire room was collapsing on itself.

"Are you ok, Ricky? You look like you're ill!" said Emma, looking at him, concerned.

"Yeah, nah, I'm alright, just need a bit of fresh air or somethin'," he said, so they paid the bill and went for a walk.

The cool evening air did help his nerves a little; he was able to breathe normally again, at least, but his heart was still pounding.

"I love this time of year!" said Emma, raising her arms like Maria von Trapp in *The Sound of Music*.

"Yeah, it's good, the evenings are cool and the days are warm, and there's a little refreshing breeze that sweeps through," replied Ricky.

"Exactly!" agreed Emma. "So... what did you want to talk to me about?"

Ricky exhaled. There was no getting out of it now.

He tried picking his words carefully, but he ended up stuttering over himself a little as he tried to grasp for them.

"I, ah, yeah, yeah I did. I just wanted to tell you that I had a really good time in Byron..." he began.

"Me too, Ricky! Honestly, you surprised me a little at how willing you were to take on Guru Naimki's teachings."

"Yeah, yeah. I think I enjoyed it cus of you... I, ah, you mean a lot to me, Emma," he stumbled over himself. He felt like an idiot, like a stunned mullet that'd just been shot by a spear gun.

But Emma understood what he was trying to say and she smiled gently.

"I like you too, Ricky."

Ricky's heart was pounding at this point, he couldn't believe how it was going.

"But..." began Emma, and Ricky's stomach dropped.

"I just don't know about it all... love was never my strongest characteristic."

"Wasn't ever mine either, but I reckon I could learn..."

Emma smiled. "Well, I reckon we could try learning it together then."

They were at her door by then and she leant and kissed him on the cheek. "Goodnight, Ricky."

Ricky smiled, feeling as light as a cloud floating lazily in the summer sky. "Night, Emma."

Ricky almost skipped home that night. He burst through his front door excitedly and cheered to himself. He couldn't stop smiling at himself when he brushed his teeth in the mirror, and when he finally lay down to sleep his heart felt full of joy.

10

Two weeks passed. Ricky had started officially working at the café, and he and Emma had met up more frequently. They went for walks mostly. Something about being outdoors and moving around made things feel less tense and formal, and helped them both relax a little. In truth, Emma had been just as surprised as Ricky was to find out that they'd both felt the same about one another. She knew that she needed time for things to grow. Not too long before she'd had her heart crushed by her first love. It took her what felt like an eternity to get over him, and although she had, she wondered if she would ever get over the idea of their love. She'd thought it was so innocent and beautiful, it was hard to move on from that, but she knew she had to so that she could grow.

Their budding relationship took its first test when Emma invited Ricky to one of her artist friends' parties in Surry Hills. He agreed, but he wasn't looking forward to it. Ricky hated arty people, not because of their art, but because of their egos. It never made sense to him why so many artistic people had such a 'fuck you' attitude, as if it was them against the world. It was so easy to be creative nowadays; everyone supported you and your ideas and everyone respected people who follow their dreams. Today, if someone believed in themselves enough they could drop out of university and chase their dreams of becoming a musician, artist or filmmaker, and their family and friends would most likely support them fully. Back when Ricky was growing up, if you dropped out of university to become an artist you'd be eaten alive by your family and peers. It really was a 'me against the world' mentality then, because society was against the people that refused to conform to its expectations. They were the pioneers that suffered immensely for their vision, and the creatives of today never gave gratitude for it, in his view. The creatives of today could be who they were because of the struggle of those first radicals. Ricky couldn't stand the edgy people in Newtown, because they acted like their ideas were too crazy for the world as they commuted to their art school funded by their parents and supported by their peers. He reckoned those kinds of creatives were full of shit, and they tried to hide how boring they really were behind hair dye and wacky clothes. If there was one type of person Ricky couldn't stand, it was phoneys. He didn't think he was anything much, in fact he mostly disliked his qualities, but he knew that at least he was real.

Emma naturally disagreed with this, and argued that it wasn't a 'fuck you' attitude, but a mode of self-expression that couldn't be put into words, so instead it came out wacky and weird. Ricky didn't argue with her – in reality he was nervous to go to the party because it was a world he'd never experienced before. His parties were backyard ones around a barbeque and a stained-glass table. His friends' kids would be causing a ruckus, and every now and then one of his mates would pull their son in for a hug and say, "Go and get ya dad a beer, would ya?"

The thought of going to an artsy party scared him; it made him feel like a small fish that'd just swum out into the wide openness of the ocean.

The party wasn't as scary as Ricky expected, and the artsy people he met were mostly nice at first. The food was good. He hung around the snack bar for most of the night, munching on the cheese and crackers and grabbing a beer from the ice bucket that sat next to it whenever he was thirsty. He was trying to be on his best behaviour – he knew it was a big step for Emma to invite him to a party like that, and even though they hadn't so much as kissed yet he felt like they were slowly taking steps in the right direction.

At one point, he tried making conversation with some of the people in the party, but he quickly regretted it. Either he felt like he couldn't keep up with the conversation, or the conversation was about nothing but the speaker. In fact, most of the people talking were talking about themselves. There was so much chatter around him, and it seemed to him that everyone was talking, but no one was listening.

After that realisation, he felt uncomfortable. People would ask him questions about what he did, or where he lived and he became embarrassed. After one or two times of telling someone he worked as a dishwasher at a café, he decided it'd make him sound better if he just told them he was taking a break from work, to which they'd nod appreciatively as if to say, 'Good for you.'

Ricky felt like an eyesore, but what was worse was that it made him feel worlds away from Emma. She belonged with these people, because they were free and uncaring of what the world thought about them. He was stuck in his ways, and he felt as if he'd only bring her down from the graceful individual she was.

He went to go and find her. She was off somewhere talking with friends and he figured he'd probably be better off by her side, but when he found her she was alone with a man. They were talking in the corner of the kitchen. She was leaning on the kitchen bench and he was standing, and they were very close. They were in an intense conversation, and as the man spoke Emma put her hand through her hair, and then grabbed his arm and laughed. That was enough for Ricky. He couldn't be there any more. He imagined what Codge and the boys back at the Crystal Castle would say if they were there. They'd have started a fight by then, he figured, and he made a mental note not to tell them about it. He felt anger, pain and jealousy all at once, and the concoction of emotions sunk down in his stomach, hot and heavy. But most of all he felt embarrassed. He was embarrassed that he thought that he and Emma could have been anything more than friends.

The old him would have tried to fight the man, but the fire within him for fighting had been extinguished. He had been disarmed by love, and now he felt as if he was paying the price.

He walked to Wynyard from Surry Hills after the party. He could have easily jumped on a train or a bus, but he felt like the walk would do him good. It was a cool night. Winter was finally approaching, and Ricky walked with his coat done up fully. It was around nine-thirty and the city was bustling with people lining up to get into clubs and bars, or just wandering the streets yelling loudly in their drunken states. He chuckled to himself as he watched a couple of boys get thrown out of a pub and stumble off into the darkness. It was funny seeing people in stages of life that he used to be in. Ricky smiled because those boys reminded him of himself, and he laughed because looking at himself from the outside suddenly made every problem he thought he had funny. He liked the atmosphere of city nights because he felt like he was able to slip by unnoticed, and he was able to people-watch as he made his way to the bus. That was one thing that he hated about the beaches. Everyone knew one another and it was impossible to go anywhere without bumping into someone. He liked feeling as if he was just another face in the crowd.

He hopped on a bus at Wynyard. He tried to look out of the window, but it was mostly dark outside, and often when there were no street lamps he'd end up just staring into his own reflection. Something about sitting on public transport makes people think. The world passes by outside the window, and the wind is blocked off and silenced, and above the roaring engine of the bus all that can be heard are thoughts. Ricky was thinking about Emma. He felt like an idiot. Their age gap was too big and he knew it from the start, and he hated himself for having slipped so far into his feelings.

His phone vibrated in his pocket, and he leant over to pull it out. It was Emma calling him. He breathed out and tried to answer naturally. "Hey, Emma, how's it goin'?"

"Ricky! Where are you? I've been looking everywhere for you," she said. There was laughter and chatter in the background; she was obviously still at the party.

"Yeah, nah, I'm on the bus home at the moment. Wasn't feelin' so good," he said.

"Oh no! You should have said goodbye! I would have come back with you," said Emma.

A pulse of anger flashed through Ricky. "Nah, it's all good – I didn't wanna disturb you and that bloke in the kitchen..."

Emma paused for a moment. "Disturb? What do you mean?"

"Nah, just looked like you were gettin' close is all," said Ricky.

"Close? How dare you, Ricky? What, do you think I'd just do something like that? You know me better than that…"

"Yeah, nah, you're right, but, yeah, that's why I didn't come say goodbye," he said. He didn't want to argue with her, and he felt even more foolish.

"Where are you going now then?" asked Emma.

"Pub. Need to have a beer," said Ricky.

"Ok, well I'm coming too," stated Emma matter-of-factly, and before Ricky could reply she hung up.

"Fuck sake…" Ricky said to himself, and a moment later he was back to watching the world pass by outside the window.

11

"Look who it is!" said Codge when Ricky walked through the pub door. "Aye, thought you'd forgotten us, big dog, left the boys for that girl," he continued. His face was bright red and his words were slurred.

"Ah, fuck off, cunt," said Ricky, clasping him on the shoulder. But Codge really was annoyed with Ricky. He hated it when his mates dogged him, especially for a woman. He was of the understanding that they'd all been through enough heartbreak in their lives to realise that companionship with women paled in comparison to mateship, and for Ricky to just leave for a few weeks without so much as a goodbye sat with Codge in a bad way. The rest of the boys didn't care, and they greeted Ricky the same as they'd always done, but Codge remained cold.

"She's comin' here tonight, so you'll get to meet her," said Ricky.

"Are you fuckin' serious?" Codge replied angrily. "Mate, this is a fuckin' sanctuary for the boys, I thought we'd all agree on that."

"Come on, Codge, mate, you can't meet her one time? You're at this pub every night, it's not like I'm gonna start bringing her here every day..."

"Yeah? That's where it starts. This time it was a couple of weeks, next time you'll be gone for months, and you reckon you could just walk back in like you hadn't just dogged the boys? We're your mates, we've fuckin' been here for you through everything, and you leave us for some chick?"

"Fuckin' hell, Codgey. What, I can't go on a holiday? Course you've been here for me, so have I for you."

Damo changed the subject in an attempt to lighten the mood. "Oi, how's this? Apprentice fell through the roof today on site, right through all the plasterboard and that!"

The group laughed and the mood was lifted a little, and all the boys around the table began sharing their funniest building-site stories, and although they'd heard them all a hundred times before, they'd listen to them again as if it was the first time.

Ricky's favourite was one of Damo's about this family that lived in an apartment block. They went on a two-week holiday, and instead of giving their dog to a friend to mind they left two weeks' worth of dog food in a big pile for the dog to eat. Obviously, the poor boy ate all the food within the first day or two, and after a week it jumped off the balcony because it could smell food in one of the other apartments and died. It was an awful story, but it was so bad it was good, and Ricky couldn't help but laugh when he heard it.

Codge always told a story about how his boss felt sorry for a homeless man, and gave him some work helping him renovate his house. Most of the work involved getting in the roof and laying air-conditioning ducts. It was hard labour, but the man worked well and Codge's boss ended up really liking the man. That was until one morning when the boss's wife was having a shower and noticed the homeless man was above her in the roof peeping through the air-conditioning vent. He'd been doing it every morning without fail for almost two weeks, and the boss had no choice but to kick him out of the house.

Some crazy things happened on building sites. Construction workers worked in so many different houses and they got exposed to different people's worlds every day, and some of those people were stranger than others.

Ricky and his mates had all worked on building sites and in factories since they were young. They knew no other kinds of work besides what they started at eighteen.

All the people like them left school and went to work- in the mines and the dark holes, they worked, in giant fridges and factories they worked, out in the sun, they worked, while the heat burned their skin and turned it to saggy leather. They smoked all day as an excuse to take a break and as a result, it became more than a habit but a part of their inner ritual. Just as a religious man prays for better days, the working man waited impatiently for smoko.

Like a doctor handles his utensils the working man fiddled with rolling papers and filters while they carefully rolled their cigarettes.

It was their numbers that gave them power- even the foreman and the managers smoked. It was one of those things that brought everyone together, pinching people's cigarettes and asking one another for lighters.

Boys that finished school and started at these places learned to work quickly. They lived on meat pies and chocolate milk, they listened to rock music on blown-out speakers, and every day they covered themselves in dirt and grime, sweat and filth. Most of them had recurring injuries before their early thirties. No one took care of themselves. If the site was full of toxic dust and chemicals no one wore a mask, if someone was grinding metal that sparked and sprayed metal shards, no one wore goggles. The last thing anyone wanted to look like was a pussy. It was the dumbest thing about the culture because so many of them lived in pain and refused to do anything about it. Proud or ignorant, you can call them what you want, but you'd never understand unless you worked in those conditions. If you were to wear a mask when no one else was, was to imply that you valued yourself over them.

Just as if you stopped working because it was too hot, or the conditions of the job were too dangerous, someone else would take your place and do it for you, and that was a shame above all else.

Forty minutes later Emma walked through the door. Ricky really didn't want her to be there; it was far too dingy a place for her, and he reckoned it would most likely be a rude shock after being at her friend's party.

She smiled when she saw him, but it was less warm than usual. Things were still tense after their phone call and Ricky almost scrambled up when she arrived at the table.

"Boys, this is Emma, Emma, this is Codgey and Damo," said Ricky as he pulled out a chair for Emma.

"Hello Codgey and Damo, it's nice to meet you finally. Ricky's told me a lot about you," said Emma.

Codgey laughed. "Fuck me, hopefully good things!"

Emma laughed. "Of course!"

Emma constantly surprised Ricky. As soon as she sat down she engaged both Codge and Damo in conversation, asking them both what they did for work and if they liked it, and if they had families and so on.

The boys acted strangely at first; they weren't used to being around a girl like Emma. She radiated beauty and patience. Codge's wife had lost patience with him a long time ago, and to him she was far from beautiful. Her soft, kind features had turned stone cold to him, lined with distrust and constant anger. He was terrified of her – she'd slap him around and boss him all over the place, but as much as they argued and bickered he loved her and needed her more than anything else in his life. They used to laugh at him when he'd come to the pub after fighting with his wife, saying, "Where's ya collar, mate? Your missus finally let you out of the doghouse?"

But sooner or later the other boys either got divorced, or their relationships had deteriorated in the exact same way, and they stopped laughing at Codge. Instead they all hid out together, dreading the time when they had to go home and face the wrath of their wives.

Once Codge and Damo had become more comfortable with Emma around they opened up a little more.

"So whaddya think of Byron, mate?" Damo asked Ricky before taking a sip from his beer.

"Fuck that place, got king hit on the first day! Chinese was alright but…" laughed Ricky. He decided to share a little more, hoping that it was the right decision. "But Emma here took me to a guru and showed me a little bit about meditation and that, and how to be thankful of the stuff in your life."

"Yeah? Has it worked?" asked Damo. Damo was surprisingly open-minded for a guy that dressed like he was ready to punch on at any moment. He was never sarcastic, unlike Codge, who almost choked on his beer at the mention of meditation.

"Fuck off! Meditation? You?" blurted out Codge, as if trying to piece a puzzle together.

"Yeah, mate, you should try it. I'm startin' to feel a little better about everything," said Ricky, almost confrontationally.

"Fair dinkum..." replied Codge, emptying his glass.

They sat around the table for a while, laughing and drinking, and the boys started to warm up to Emma. Ricky was relieved that Emma wasn't repulsed by his friends. He didn't think they were exactly her type, and they were planets away from her friends back at the party in the city. Ricky was happy that Emma had come, but he still wanted to ask her about the man she was chatting with at the party. All he wanted to know was that Emma didn't prefer the other guy, and that she hadn't only come to the pub to see him because she'd felt bad he'd caught her. He'd seen girls talk like that, running their hands through their hair with plenty of eye contact. It was a look he hadn't seen in many years, but it was an unmistakable flirtatiousness that he used to search for almost desperately at parties. The thought of Emma flirting with that guy made him feel insecure, and he looked at her differently than he had before. He'd only ever seen her alone, and the thought never occurred to him that maybe she had other guys who were interested in her too. It made sense to him – she was the most beautiful woman he'd ever seen, and his stomach turned when he thought of the kinds of guys that would be interested in her too.

He stood up and went to the bathroom. He could feel himself slipping away into his head and he needed a breather. It took all of his effort to calm himself down. Ricky's mind had always been like a rolling ball of entropy, constantly drawing him to destructive thoughts and actions. So much so that he found comfort when he was at his lowest, because that feeling was familiar to him. He'd lived most of his life in the pits of his mind, and he felt safe there. When he felt himself feeling happy again he became scared, because this mind state was alien to him, and he knew that eventually he'd have to take a dive again. There's nothing in life that can't be taken away, so you may as well live like you have nothing to give. That was Ricky's logic, anyways.

Ricky stood in a toilet cubicle for a while, trying to pull himself out of the downwards spiral that was taking place in his head. After a few minutes he knew he needed to go back. He felt bad leaving Emma at the table by herself, so he took a couple of deep breaths and left the toilet.

Ricky found his way back to the table and sat back down, but before he had a chance to say anything Alph roared from across the bar. He had strolled into the pub wearing a loose-buttoned shirt that revealed a bright red chest, burned to a crisp in the Thailand sun.

"Here he is!" roared Codge, and Alph raised both his arms to the ceiling as if he'd just won a boxing match.

"How was it? You get any birds?" asked Codge. It was as if he'd instantly forgotten Emma was at the table.

"Did I get any birds? Mate, I was fuckin' multiple birds a day! They're so cheap over there, and so young-lookin'!" Alph replied excitedly, his face a few shades redder than usual.

"You're fucked!" laughed Damo.

Emma was repulsed, and even Ricky felt a little uneasy.

"Nah, fuck off, there was one night I even had two of 'em at once!"

"Fuck me dead, when are we all goin' over, boys? I'm bookin' my flight tomorrow," said Codge.

"Dead set..." Damo agreed, and then they looked to Ricky expectantly.

Ricky shook his head. "Nah, I'm good, boys, more for you then."

Alph cocked his head. "Nah? What are ya, fuckin' gay?" Alph took no notice of Emma sitting there as he stood over Ricky, swaying a little from intoxication.

"Not gay, mate, just not interested..." said Ricky.

Alph couldn't believe his ears. "Not interested? Fuck me, you go and fall in love with some girl and all of a sudden you've gone all soft on us!" He pointed at Emma as he spoke.

"Fuck off, cunt..." said Ricky, standing up.

"No, Ricky, it's fine!" said Emma, grabbing his arm.

"Ah yeeaahh, there ya go! Oh no, Ricky, it's fine!" said Alph in a mocking tone. "Fuck me, Rick, what happened to you mate?"

He knew what he was doing. If he got Ricky angry enough he'd take a swing, and Emma would see who the real Ricky was. He was angry at Ricky; it was as if Ricky was acting like he was better than them, like he'd never been to the brothel with them, or gotten a late-night massage with them after a night out.

Ricky didn't take a swing. Instead he felt embarrassed with himself. Here he was acting like he'd changed after a few weeks just because a girl had come into his life, and all of a sudden, he was turning on his mates. And even though he wanted to change, he wanted to agree with Emma, he cracked under the peer pressure.

Emma tried to pull him away from the table. Like Alph she thought he'd take a swing too, but Ricky stood fixed to the ground.

"Come on, Ricky, they're not worth it," she said, soothingly.

But Ricky resisted her this time, he could feel all eyes on the table watching him, studying his every move silently, waiting to see what he would do next.

"They're not worth it? Well, those are my friends, they're the realest blokes you'd ever meet, not like that fuckin' guru cunt that sits on waterfalls... What a fuckin' joke. The only thing he was missin' was a crystal ball," shouted Ricky. He was drunk and angry and felt desperate to win his friends' respect back.

Emma looked at him, pained, as if he'd just shoved a dagger through her heart. "How dare you...? I took you there so that maybe you would open up a bit to the world, to yourself! I did that for you!"

"Ah, get fucked! You did that cus you felt sorry for me, and you felt sorry for yourself. I wonder how it'd feel never workin' a day in your fuckin' life? Does it get borin' doin' fuck all, make you feel like you gotta meddle in someone else's life?"

Emma was speechless. He had hurt her badly. Without another word she turned and stormed out of the pub.

"Christ, Ricky..." said Damo, "you've gone and fucked that one up!"

"Ah, fuck off, cunt!" spat Ricky, and he stormed out of the pub too.

Ricky didn't make it home after he left the pub. He went to the beach and jumped into the water. He needed to feel it wash over him, and float in it for a while. He wasn't worried about sharks, he'd always reckoned daytime and nighttime were pretty much the same thing to a shark, it was twilight and dawn you had to watch out for. It was a calm night, and as he waded out into the water he lifted his arms above the gentle swells that rolled past him. He dove under the water and opened his eyes and saw nothing but darkness around him from all angles. It was a strangle feeling, floating within the darkness. He pictured himself and Emma at the pub so vividly in his head that it was as if the image had projected itself into the dark waters in front of him. He was thinking of her face. Every feature seemed to twist and contort in pain and hurt because of what he'd said to her. He'd thrown her away because of foolish pride. A deep shame sunk into his stomach as he floated under the water, and a shiver ran down his spine. A moment later he was above the surface again, gasping for air.

He didn't like diving into the dark, and he decided he was better off just floating above the surface for a while. The sky was clear, and as he floated on his back he lost himself in the universe, floating peacefully over a sea of stars reflected below him.

"Praise be," he said, after spending some time in silence. It felt right to give thanks, at least for the ocean and the sky.

12

The next day he woke up late with a raging headache. But his stomach was the thing that pained him most. He couldn't rid himself from the shame that hung in it so heavily; it felt as if he'd swallowed a couple of dumbbells.

What was worse was that he'd spent so much money over the last few weeks that his savings were almost completely gone. Between the holiday to Byron and general life expenses he hadn't left much room to save. He'd never learned how to save money properly when he was a kid because he never saw much of it growing up. His mum gave him a roof over his head, and worked overtime so that he had food on his plate, but they were stuck in a continuous cycle of existence. He never learned how to invest or how to save, and it was a gap in his knowledge to that day. He would get his paycheque each week and spend it on beers, food and petrol for his car, and the rest of it would be used up for his rent and bills. He hadn't been getting much money from the biscuit factory anyway, just a little over minimum wage. He couldn't imagine how hard it would be to have a kid of his own. He felt like he could barely keep himself alive, let alone another human being. He almost resented people he knew that came from privileged families, not because he was jealous of their wealth, but because of their lack of understanding for life outside of their position. When he was in his early twenties some of his old friends were from rich families. They were the least generous people too. He'd come up short paying for food and instead of helping him out they'd embarrass him, or they'd rinse him afterwards and ask, "Man, where does all your money go? It's like you're broke all the time, don't you save at all?"

It used to infuriate him. He grew up with little, and had had to work since he was fourteen. He worked almost every day after school and on the weekends, and as soon as he was eighteen he had to fend for himself. Those same friends were in their early twenties living at home with no expenses except for what they did for leisure, and they were lecturing him about saving. On the other hand, his friends from families like his were generous, and although they had little in the way of money they were always willing to share it around and help one another out. It was a brotherhood of the less fortunate; they accepted one another for everything that they were because they had little ego and low expectations. He'd had to work hard his whole life, and he felt like he had nothing to show for it except a chip on his shoulder and an unreassuring savings account.

Emma was twenty-six years old. She'd travelled a lot since she finished school. She'd been all around Europe, Asia, North and South America and parts of the Middle East too. She'd experienced a lot over those years travelling: culture, traditions, religions, but mostly she'd learned to be empathetic with people. She'd never forgotten her pilgrimage to India. When she'd first awakened her desire to discover her own spirituality she'd packed her bags and headed on a spiritual pilgrimage to all of the significant yogi temples.

She'd read so much about the beauty and elegance of Indian culture, but when she got there she was stunned at the level of extreme poverty. It was heartbreaking to her. She met some fellow Australians like herself who were also on a spiritual pilgrimage. The temples were beautiful, elegant, and rich with culture and wisdom, just as she'd read in her books. And as she and the other spiritual pilgrims gathered in these places and prayed for world peace, and love and oneness of everything, she couldn't shake the thought that just outside of the temple walls there was agony and chaos. She saw limbless women and children begging next to the temple steps, the ill and injured writhing in pain, all while she and her yogi friends prayed for the world just thirty metres away, separated only by the temple walls.

That became a driving force for her to make changes in her life. She had been blessed her entire life. She'd come from an extremely wealthy, loving and caring family, and she felt like the only way that she could feel blessed was to pass on blessings to others.

After she came home from India, she apologized to her parents. She'd been a nightmare growing up. She and her father would fight constantly, to the point where after she'd finished school she stopped talking to him completely. After seeing so much depravity in the world, she was embarrassed by it all, and ashamed at herself for how she'd behaved. Her father had his issues, but he was a considerate and fair man, although hotheaded and impatient at times. She'd never forgotten what her father said to her after their last argument before she left the house and moved out. It was the biggest argument they'd ever had, she couldn't even remember what it was about, most likely it was just a boiling point after weeks of tension. After ten minutes of yelling at each other back and forth she told him that she hated him.

He tried to keep his composure, but she had hurt him to the core, she could see it in his eyes.

But instead of yelling, which is what she'd expected him to do, he said quietly, "Just be thankful you live in a world where you are allowed to hate me, even though I love you."

She stormed off after he'd said that. She wasn't angry but embarrassed, ashamed of herself. She was in the wrong and she knew it, and she hated that.

13

The next day Ricky was driving through the countryside alone. It was a sunny Sunday, and before he had to go back and work at the café he felt like he needed to clear his mind a little. He didn't really have a destination in particular, he just felt like listening to music and watching the world go past as he drove. It was a mostly warm day, but the wind had the slightest chill in it, which was Ricky's favourite weather. Warm enough that he could feel the touch of the sun, but not too hot, and if he liked he could wear a light jumper without overheating.

He drove for an hour or so before he stopped at the side of a massive bridge that the highway crossed over. He got out of his car and looked over the edge at the calm creek far below. When there were no cars passing he could hear the sound of the water gurgling over the rocks below and echoing through the valley. He liked this place. Instead of driving any further he locked his car and went looking for a bush trail that led down to the creek. He found one after a few minutes and began his descent. He was happy he had stopped; the walk was beautiful. All he could hear as he walked were birds of all different kinds of species. There was a bird on each side of him, and when the two called to one another it sounded like a laser beam was being shot past him. It took him some time before he finally got to the bottom, and at that point he was out of breath and tired. He eyed the path again, not looking forward to when he had to walk back up.

The creek was cool and breathless, shrouded by trees that blocked out most of the sunlight. Instead light beamed down through the gaps in the branches here and there like natural spotlights. He found himself a place in the sun and settled down. It was nice down there. He sat for a while watching the flowing water, or cleaning the dirt out of his fingernails. It was the first time he'd felt happy to be alone. He felt connected to it all. He imagined himself standing over the creek with a spear in his hand, waiting to strike any fish he saw travelling downstream. That would be a good life, he thought. Catching fish and bringing them back to a family. Sitting by the fire on dark lonely nights, and dancing in the moonlight when the moon was full. He closed his eyes and listened to everything around him, and as he listened he took a deep breath and exhaled.

Emma hadn't spoken to him since their fight at the bar a few nights before. He hadn't messaged her since, even though he desperately wanted to. He was scared of what she'd say. A lot of his time driving that day was spent reliving that argument and trying to change it in his head. Or he'd imagine them having another argument, but this time he was in the right and he was winning. He came up with so many good points, but he knew in person he'd be left hopelessly trying to grasp for any words that came to his mouth.

He needed to come clean. He needed to tell her that he loved her.

She'd shown him so much love and compassion, so much patience and understanding, and he'd tried as best he could to change for her, but he had been moulded by his lifestyle for so long he felt brittle and inflexible.

He got back to Sydney that evening, and after staring at his phone for a while in silence he finally dialled up Emma's number and called it.

The anticipation was torturous, and every ring seemed to echo louder in his head.

The phone rang a few times before she finally picked up. "Hello?"

"Hey, how are you goin'?" asked Ricky.

"Good, and you?" said Emma, coldly.

"Yeah, good... I, ah, I'm sorry, Emma," Ricky began, he could feel his heart thumping against his chest, and all of a sudden his mouth became very dry. "I didn't mean any of the things I said that night. I just caved in to the pressure and I feel like a fuckin' idiot. Honestly, you've brought so much joy into my life again, and I feel ashamed that I let you down like that."

"I understand, but how could you say those things to me? And how could you think that I just spent time with you because I felt sorry for you?"

"I know... I'm sorry," said Ricky. "Can we meet at the headland? I wanna talk to you in person."

Emma paused for a moment, it felt like a lifetime to Ricky, but she finally said, "Ok."

Half an hour later Ricky and Emma met at the headland. It was a tense few initial moments, and the gap between them physically felt enormous.

"Hey..." said Ricky.

But Emma remained silent, she was waiting for what Ricky had to say to her.

After a few moments, Ricky exhaled. "I'm sorry, Emma, I don't know what else I can say."

She said nothing.

Ricky was silent for a while too, and the pair just stood there looking out into the horizon.

"I feel so stupid, Emma, because," he caught himself before he said it, and the air hung onto his words, "because I love you."

He'd never felt so vulnerable in his life, sitting there waiting for Emma to respond.

She smiled like she always smiled, with care and love, but there was no longer a spark of romantic tension. Instead it felt like the love and care of a mother or sister.

"I love you too, Ricky. But I know now that we could never work. You've taught me a lot, and I'm thankful for that."

Ricky's heart dropped, but he understood. "Yeah, I've learned a lot from you too." He knew now that it could never be.

Emma smiled at him and kissed him on the cheek before standing and leaving him sitting by the headland. He was devastated to watch her walk away.

He sat there for a while and looked out into the horizon. He watched the birds darting through the air, and the clouds drifting slowly above him, and he closed his eyes and listened to all that was around him. She would never love him like he loved her, but she had made him feel like a man again, and he was thankful for that.

He opened his eyes, took a deep breath and whispered to himself, "Praise be…"

He knew that it had to end. Until just a few weeks ago, Emma had not been in his life at all. It was a twist of fate that they'd ever come to meet. Ricky imagined their lives like two parallel beams of light travelling side by side, and for a split second the beams of light collided with one another and travelled as one, until they finally split and went on their separate paths. He wasn't sure if they'd ever collide again, and a part of him hoped they wouldn't. Some people are better off left in the memory, unchanged forever to be visited in daydreams.

Ricky had come to realise he was a great romanticist; he'd just never allowed himself to think like that before. His entire life had been governed by the emotions of love and loss. They were the two basic human experiences that he could share with anyone, even the blokes he and the boys had beaten up at the pub a few weeks before.

And even though it'd been hard, Ricky was thankful for everything that had happened because it forced him to take the steps towards changing himself for the better.

He enjoyed the work at the café, he still managed to swim every day, and he drank less and less.

A few days later he was at the supermarket doing his weekly shop. He'd found a healthy eating guide on the internet and printed it out for his shopping list. Carrots, broccoli and all kinds of fruits were thrown into his basket. He felt proud of himself as he walked up and down the aisles, turning packets over and reading their ingredient lists. He'd been thinking about getting a gym membership too, but that was another challenge for another time, he wasn't going to run before he could crawl.

To his surprise, halfway down the healthcare aisle he bumped into Phillip. He was wearing a buttoned high-vis shirt, steel-capped boots, and his sleeves were rolled up to his elbows.

"Well, looks like God did find ya a job!" said Ricky.

Phillip turned around and smiled when he saw it was Ricky.

"Ricky, mate! How you been? And yeah, I got a job workin' in the mines! Just finished my first training day, then we're headin' out to Newcastle next week."

"Ah, fuck yeah, Phillip, good on ya, mate!" said Ricky, slapping him on the back.

"How about you? Have you found yourself another job?" asked Phillip.

"Yeah, actually, just washin' dishes at a café at the moment," Ricky replied.

Phillip's lips curled into a wry smile. Ricky working a shitkicker job was the best news he'd heard all day.

He'd thought a lot about Ricky since the pair of them had been let go from the biscuit factory. Ricky had been the cause of so much anger and frustration in his life. Phillip was a good man, and he gave Ricky more respect than he had deserved. Ricky was a lazy, uncaring and unmotivated slob, and the worst part was that the whole time they had worked together Ricky had always made Phillip feel small.

But now the tables had turned, and Phillip had just the response waiting for Ricky.

"Damn, Ricky, maybe you should have tried praying for a better job..."

Ricky laughed at the irony and felt a swell of pride in him that Phillip no longer annoyed him so much. He put his hand on Phillip's shoulder, looked him dead in the eye and said, "Get fucked, Phil."

The End

PRAISE BE

E.H.

www.ingramcontent.com/pod-product-compliance
Lightning Source LLC
Chambersburg PA
CBHW020226120726
47903CB00008B/2568